Of Murders and Mages

Nikki Haverstock

DEDICATION

To my amazing editor Jodi Henley who held me hand
through countless rewrites.

CONTENTS

CHAPTER ONE

I pushed the elevator button for our floor with enough force to hurt my finger. I never should have agreed to take a trip with Norman. I thought it would be a fun weekend in Rambler, Nevada—or as they liked to advertise it, "Vegas if they had never gone family-friendly." I had never been that fond of Norman, but I couldn't turn down a free trip. But after a few days trapped with him, I didn't even want to look at him. Even the sound of his breathing through his mouth made me want to rip my skin off.

The elevator doors opened, and I surged into the hallway, heading toward our room. In twelve hours, I would be home and would never see him again. Quickly, I realized that this wasn't our floor but appeared to be under construction and dark. Why hadn't I noticed before I exited?

"Ethel, this isn't our floor," Norman said behind me, his mouth hanging open.

"Obviously not, Einstein." I huffed. The bare structure of support beams dotted the floor where there were rooms on our floors. A missing window to my right was covered in thin plastic that flapped in the wind.

"The elevator's gone."

"Well, push the button and get us to our room. I just want to pack and go to bed." I couldn't even stand to look in Norman's

1

direction as my eyes adjusted to the dark floor.

"No, the entire thing is gone—no door, no button, nothing."

"Don't be an idiot." A chill passed over me, and I rubbed my arms and shook my head. Perhaps the third glass of wine had been a bad idea, as it churned in my stomach and threatened to come back up.

"Momma?" a thin, hesitant voice cut through the darkness.

It had been more than thirty years since I had heard that voice. My son's voice, my only child, my baby. He had died of whooping cough and couldn't be here.

"Momma!"

It was his voice and cut straight through me. It was coming from the open window. I plowed through the construction rubble, something digging into my shin, but I felt no pain. I could hear my son's breathing in my ears and smell his toddler hair. He was here and real.

"Where are you going?" Norman shouted behind me, his voice thin and unreal, as if I were hearing it underwater.

I shoved the plastic aside from the window, the sparkling neon lights of Rambler in front of me and a chilly wind whipping around me. I extended a hand, and firm in my grip was my son's chubby hand. The lights and wind around me died to nothing.

"Momma, come!" His voice was stronger now. He was healthy and vibrant and his voice still twisted my heart. He tugged on my hand.

I braced a foot on the window and pushed up then took a step toward him, feeling weightless. His tiny cuddly body filled my arms, and I buried my face in his neck. His giggles filled my ears as wind raced by.

CHAPTER TWO

"Miss Ramono?"

I covered my yawn as I arched my back and stretched my neck side to side. For the past month, I had been tormented by exhausting and disturbing dreams I could barely remember in the morning. This was my first freelance job, and I was determined to knock it out of the park. I turned around to address whoever was interrupting my work.

"I'm in the middle—" I managed to hide my gasp at the towering man filling the doorframe of the small office the casino had provided for me. He had light-brown hair cropped close and icy-blue eyes that were narrowed in a suspicious squint. His wide shoulders filled the doorframe, and he radiated an animalistic energy that pushed the walls in close around me.

"They want to know if you are any relation to Ramono the Bull." His deep, gravelly voice dragged out the words. He was younger than I initially thought. The scowl etched into his face aged him, but when he relaxed briefly, his skin was smooth except for the five-o'clock shadow.

"Yes, he was my father." A deep wave of sorrow passed through me as the past tense twisted in my stomach. Even three years later, I could barely say he was gone without tearing up.

"Don't lie." The angry giant in the doorway narrowed his eyes again.

Of course, if I thought a man was handsome, he was guaranteed to be a jerk. "I wouldn't lie. James Ramono the third was my father."

"He didn't have a daughter, only a son."

Anger flared in my chest. It was a familiar friend and comfort after the pain of missing my father. It must have shown in my face because the man's glare disappeared, and his face went unreadable as I stood. "Then I must be a man because my father only had one child, and it's me. Now, the casino is paying me good money to work by the hour, and I don't intend to waste my time arguing about my deceased father. Is there anything else you need?"

I was letting my emotions get away from me. My therapist would have advised that I count to five or take a deep, slow breath, but it felt good to rip into this douchewaffle that was questioning my own knowledge of my father. My cheeks were hot, and a trickle of sweat ran down my back.

The man's eyes widened briefly, and he nodded before leaving the room without another word. The door stood open behind him.

I took a moment to breathe in over a count of five, hold the breath, then let it out slowly over another count of five, and my temperature started to drop. It had been a bizarre encounter, but that was Rambler. A city I was still struggling to understand since I moved into Dad's loft after his murder.

Closing the door, as required by my contract since I was inspecting very important financial statements, I pushed aside all thoughts of my father. I turned back to the desk I had been given and jumped.

There on the seat was that darn cat. She was gigantic, the size of a medium dog, and had green eyes just like

4

mine. "Not you again. Shoo! Go on!" I opened the door and gestured, but she just blinked at me and lay in the seat, crossing her front paws.

She had been bothering me all morning. Twice I had gone to the bathroom, carefully locking the door behind me as instructed, only to find her on my chair when I returned. She must be sneaking in when I opened the door. Anywhere else on earth, it would be weird to find a cat in a workplace, but not Rambler, Nevada. These gigantic, long-legged cats were a status symbol here, and more than one important person in town had one that followed them around like dogs. It was another thing that gave Rambler character.

I carefully picked up the cat and slowly moved toward the door. The cats were well-known to hate everyone but their owners. Tourists were warned not to try and pet them if they valued their skin intact. I didn't want to end up clawed to pieces, so I edged toward the door on my tiptoes. My hands vibrated as the cat purred and rubbed her head against me.

"Good kitty. Nice kitty." I placed her in the hallway and shut the door. I had never seen one of these cats for sale or rescue. There must be some high-price buy-in to get one, like a Birkin bag or McLaren car. It was surprising enough to see one alone, but I had no time to think about it as I turned to face my desk.

The cat stared at me from the chair.

I stared for a few seconds, trying to work out how she had gotten past me, before I walked over and scooped her up again. "Sneaky little bugger. Come on." I opened the door, stepped into the hallway, and placed the cat gently on the floor. We locked eyes as I stepped back into the room and slowly started closing the door.

A little chill ran down my back. The intelligence behind those green eyes was unsettling. The cat's eyes narrowed as the door clicked shut, as though she were contemplating her next move.

I sat back down and returned my attention to the financial sheets in front of me. When auditing a company, I liked to spend the first day just looking around. Oftentimes, something would jump out at me or seem off even if I didn't know why. When I worked for the state auditor's office, my coworkers teased me that I had financial voodoo, but the truth was that I was just good at my job and proud of it.

This was my first solo gig auditing for a company that hired me themselves, and I needed to be twice as observant. No cats could distract me.

A sharp meow punctured the silence.

I spun around, and there in the middle of the room was that darn smug cat. I could have sworn it was smiling at me, gloating. The door was still shut.

"Son of a—how did you get back in here?" I grabbed her with a soft but firm hand, but unlike the last two times, she squirmed and wiggled before sinking her sharp teeth into the meaty webbing between my left index finger and thumb.

I gritted my teeth together and growled. The pain sent an icy chill up my arm, freezing it in place before spreading through my entire body, followed closely by another chill that transformed the sharp agony into a dull ache then only a light tingling. I stepped into the hallway and fought to move my arm. The cat finally unclenched its jaw and jumped to the floor, where it turned and licked its lips. She sat up primly and wrapped her tail around her body, though the last inch of tail twitched with delight.

"What are you doing?" The man had returned and was glaring again.

I returned the look, my patience completely gone. "Dancing the cha-cha." I rubbed my left hand, which felt both hot and cold and had the pins-and-needles sensation. I flexed the fingers, and everything seemed to work, though the hand was stiff.

"You shouldn't be touching Patagonia."

6

"Is that her name? Awfully innocent name for a spawn of Satan."

Patagonia purred loudly enough for it to fill the hallway. The corners of her mouth pulled into a grin, revealing tiny pointed fangs, one of which was still tinged pink with blood from my hand. Her right eye briefly closed in a wink at me. I shook my head. The chronic insomnia and the adrenaline from the cat's attack were making me see things.

"How do you know Patagonia is a female?"

That was a good question. I was completely sure the second I had seen her that she was a she, but why? I shrugged it off. I must have caught a view of the cat's rear end at some point. People had often accused me of knowing things I shouldn't, but I was just observant. I was a firm believer that if you paid attention, you could pick up on things without realizing it.

"The lack of fuzzy balls gave her away."

He snorted, and one corner of his mouth might have twitched into a shadow of smile. "If you are done with your dancing, Miss Olivia Santini would like you to come to her office to talk."

"About what?"

He shrugged. "Please lock the door and follow me."

My palms were sweaty as I gathered up the few things I had unpacked from my messenger bag. I had only been here less than four hours, and being fired was the only reason I could think of for the owner of the casino to ask me to come to her office.

I locked the door and followed him to her office. Olivia had run this casino, The Golden Pyramid, and several others since her father committed suicide this year. Even before then, she was influential in Rambler, with her hands in a lot of projects.

As the elevator doors closed, Patagonia snaked through them and curled up at my feet. "Should she be here?" I pointed down at the cat, who looked up and meowed loudly. I rubbed at my hand, which suddenly started throbbing again.

"She's fine." He stared straight ahead at the doors until they opened, and he exited into a hall.

I stuck out my tongue at his back and followed. I adjusted the strap on my messenger bag nervously. I couldn't imagine why Olivia Santini would want to meet with me. The first thought I had had was that she wanted to give me bad news, but why her personally? Surely the woman who hired me last week could have called me up and fired me.

What if it was related to Patagonia the cat? Perhaps the video cameras caught me wrestling her into the hallway, though the timing didn't seem correct since the jerk had shown up so quickly. Perhaps I was jumping the gun thinking of him as a jerk. I tended to make knee-jerk reactions.

"I don't have all day." He stood at an open door and tapped a foot.

My knee-jerk reactions were usually right. I swept through the door.

"Ouch!" he said behind me.

I turned, and he was clutching his calf and glaring at Patagonia. She blinked and licked her paw.

I giggled and gave the cat a long look, wondering if perhaps she was smarter than the average cat. We were in a large room. A lady at a desk looked me over. She had tightly rolled short black hair, like a nest of curls. She took off her glasses, stood, and opened a door beside her desk. She leaned in for a few seconds before gesturing me over. "Miss Santini will see you, Miss Ramono. Vin, she would like you to join them as well."

So the jerk had a name. I turned around and caught his scowl as he gave his calf one last rub. As he walked over, he had a noticeable limp.

CHAPTER THREE

I stepped into the office and braced myself for whatever was coming. The office was at the top of the casino and had a wonderful view of the Avenue, Rambler's equivalent of the Vegas Strip. The office was tastefully appointed with a small sitting area, a large desk, a mixture of plotted plants, and an impressive number of bookcases. Standing behind the desk was Olivia Santini.

The pictures I had seen of her online or in the local paper did not do her justice. She had the striking beauty of a movie star. I knew she was in her early forties, but she didn't have a wrinkle in sight, not even tiny ones around the corners of her eyes. Her smooth black hair was pulled up into ponytail that made my unruly curly hair feel wild as it tried to escape from my bun. Nothing could contain the wildness of my exceedingly long red hair.

She came around the desk and extended a hand. "Pleased to meet you, Miss Romono. I'm Olivia Santini."

I shook her smooth, strong hand. "Please call me Gabriella or just Ella for short."

She gestured to a love seat and sat opposite in a wingback chair. "And call me Olivia." She looked to the door. "Vin, please join us."

I peeked over my shoulder. Vin's facial expression was blank, but the muscles in his jaw were flexing as he came over to sit in a chair next to Olivia. He perched on the edge of the chair, and it creaked under his formidable frame. The delicate design that fit her so well looked like a toy under him.

I ducked my head to hide a snicker and startled when I saw Patagonia had silently jumped onto the love seat next to me.

"Patagonia bit her," Vin said.

Olivia arched an eyebrow at him then turned and smiled at me. "Really? May I see?"

"Oh, it was barely a—holy crap." Dark-violet lines radiated from the two puncture wounds and laced up under the cuff of my long-sleeve shirt. Frantically, I unbuttoned the cuff and shoved the sleeve up to my elbow, where the lines continued to weave and lace over my entire forearm.

Olivia squealed. "How exciting!"

Vin groaned. "You've got to be kidding me."

I looked at my right hand then down at my chest, where the violet lines continued and seemed to darken. "I've been poisoned! I'm dying." I spotted an envelope opener on the desk. "Cut my arm off before it can spread!" I stood, and my head swam. Falling to my knees, I flailed for the opener before my sight went black and I pitched forward.

When I blinked my eyes open, Vin was hovering overhead, slapping my cheeks with more force than necessary. I was disoriented and unsure of what was happening.

"You okay?" He slapped me.

My brain felt like the ball inside a pinball machine. "You can stop now."

"Yeah, not a problem."

Pulling me to my feet, he walked me to a chair and let me fall into the seat with a thump. Memories flooded back to me. Pushing at my skin, I tried to wipe the lines off. I threw my arm out and turned my head away. "Quick," I said. "Maybe you can get it off at the joint. I'm too young to die."

Olivia shushed me. "You really don't know? I can't believe it." Her cool, smooth voice carried a note of surprise. She reached across and grabbed my hand. "You're just fine. Relax."

She beckoned Vin over. "Come on. You know what to do."

He reared back a little. "I'm not getting wrapped up in this."

She shook her head. "No, I'll take that responsibility."

"Fine." He took a knee and grabbed my other hand with rough fingers that were warm in my hand. A tingling sensation spread up my arm, and the lines on my arm vibrated. "None of that," he growled at me. "It has been witnessed by one."

Olivia squeezed my hand. "It has been witnessed by two." She turned toward the open office door and shouted, "Auntie, can you come in here?"

The woman with the dark curls ducked her head in the room. "It really isn't professional for you to call—Oh my! How exciting."

She raced across the room. Placing a hand on my back, she cleared her throat. "It has been witnessed by three."

Warmth spread through me, and the lines appeared to lighten. Vin dropped my hand, but the intense heat of his touch continued on my fingertips.

The older woman leaned over the back of the couch and planted a huge kiss on my cheek. "Call me Auntie Ann, my dear. I am so excited for you. I'll get everything arranged." She reached over and scratched Patagonia behind the ear before bustling back out the door.

Patagonia purred loudly and came to my side. Hopping into my lap, she circled then dug her claws into my thighs. After kneading my skin like well-risen dough, she finally

11

curled up and closed her eyes.

"Thank you, Auntie." Olivia pressed her second hand over mine and stared into my eyes. She searched for something that only she knew, and after a few seconds that dragged out into eternity, she dropped my hand and turned to Vin. "You can get out of here before you explode."

Vin pushed off the ground in one smooth move and left without a look back.

The whole interaction had been beyond bizarre. I flipped my hand over, and though the wound still tingled, the lines on my arm were only barely visible. Maybe they hadn't been as bad as I thought? I blinked hard, and phantom lines danced behind my eyelids. I shook my head. When I came into the office, I had been concerned about getting fired, and my brain was struggling to keep up with the new situation.

"What just happened? What did you—"

Olivia held up one delicate, perfectly manicured hand. "Before I explain that, would you like to know why we thought your father had only a son?"

I fought between the two ideas. Though what had just happened was completely baffling and upsetting, there was no doubt which topic was more important to me. "You know, this is not the first time that has happened. When I first moved to Rambler, I had a few people say something similar, but no one accused me of lying."

"Did Vin say you were lying?"

I nodded and pursed my lips in frustration.

"I apologize for him. He's my cousin. Auntie Ann's son, in fact. I'm trying to civilize him for corporate work, but he's stubborn. But he had a reason to assume you were lying. Your father was quite insistent that he had only had one child, a son that lived in New York with his mother."

I stared at her in shock. I had been, and still was, I suppose, a daddy's girl. Though I had gone to boarding school, we talked consistently, and he took me on grand vacations during every school break. When I graduated college and got a job in Vegas, he had visited anytime I was free. There was no way he had a son, so why had he lied? "You knew my father?"

She nodded and closely watched my face. "Yes, he worked with my father from time to time. Quiet man and kind but very... I suppose intimidating is the right word. Do you know what he did for a living?"

That definitely sounded like my father. "Uh, he never brought work home with him or thought to discuss it during vacation. I know he did freelance work for casinos. He said he helped fix problems."

Her eyes widened for a split second, and she chuckled a little in her reply. "Yes, I guess that is a good description. He fixed things." Something in her response showed that she thought the term was funny. "In a way, you followed in his footsteps. You are helping us find and hopefully fix a problem. Speaking of which..."

She got up and removed a small pile of items and a piece of paper from the top of her desk. She passed the paper to me before sitting down. A large cat with spots followed her and hopped into her lap.

"You have a cat as well? I've always wondered where people get them. I've never seen them for sale or adoption."

She gave me a small, tight smile. "Of course you haven't. I should have known something exciting was going to happen when Patagonia first came to the office. Can you give that piece of paper a once-over?"

I scanned the paper, a photocopy of a note scribbled onto a small notepad with the Golden Pyramid casino name and logo at the top. In two columns were lists of numbers. The column on the left was one- or two-digit numbers with a slash between them, and on the right were four- or five-digit numbers. The two lists didn't perfectly match. Some numbers on the left had a blank to the right, or vice-versa.

"Ella."

I looked up at her from the paper. "Yes?"

"Can you tell me what you think these numbers mean? They were found on my father's desk after his... passing." She flinched a little as she stumbled on the last word.

My heart ached for her and me. We had both lost our fathers, and she was clearly still struggling. A cloud of sadness passed behind her eyes, and I looked away as she dabbed a tissue to them.

I gave the paper another quick look before replying. "With the work I do, I wouldn't guess. I would start by—"

"No, no, I want your gut feelings. Just humor me, please."

"As long as you realize this is just a guess. I would never say anything for sure unless I could prove it in the numbers." I looked over the numbers again, but I already knew what my gut was saying. "Right off the bat, the best option is that the column on the left is dates and the right is amounts of money. They don't perfectly match up, so I would say that someone has a specific event or expenditure in mind and they are trying to figure out when something happened and how much it cost. There are exact amounts, so either they had receipts with no dates, or..." Something tickled the back of my mind, an option that wasn't fully formed.

"Close your eyes and relax." I must have hesitated, because her tone was firm when she continued. "You are working for me. Please listen when I ask you to do something."

I closed my eyes. People don't understand what I do. I follow the facts, though that didn't fully cover what I did. Sometimes the numbers reflected human nature. Repeated purchases reflect our habits. A sudden increase or decrease in a particular category could reflect a life change. I had caught many coworkers in an affair when there was a sudden increase in work-lunch-reimbursement requests. Or embezzlement schemes when every department under one person had a consistent but tiny increase in costs each month.

I opened my eyes and looked at the list. What was this list telling me? Without knowing what category the money was pulled from, it could be anything. There was no pattern to the numbers. Except...

"Not all these numbers instantly make sense, but there is one interesting pattern that I can see right off the bat." I went down the list. "There is a payment of fifty thousand dollars every month on this list on the ides."

"The ides?"

"Yes, like the ides of March, which is March fifteenth. It is a common misconception that the ides means the fifteenth, but it actually means the middle of the month in the Roman calendar, so it falls on the fifteenth of March, May, July, or October, and the thirteenth of the rest of the months. See." I passed her the list.

She ran a hand down the list. "So the fifteenth of March, May..."

"July and October," I offered.

She nodded. "That makes sense. I did notice the payments, and they happened monthly around the time, but I didn't understand why it jumped between the fifteenth and thirteenth."

I nodded. "It is one of those funny little facts that stuck in my head. The same way that I remember that the lady who jumped from your casino did it on May fifteenth. Poor woman. That was so sad."

Olivia looked at the list again. "Yes, you're right. In fact..." She muttered to herself and ran a finger down the list. Her eyes darted back to me. "You're very good."

She passed me back the paper. "Please keep thinking on it a bit more. I have something else for you." She handed me a cool white stone the size of my palm and shaped like an egg. "Look at this. Can you see the colors in it?"

I tucked the paper into my bag then turned my attention to the stone. It was a milky white and super smooth. I flipped it over in my hand, and a creamy glow rose from the stone. It was like the shimmer of moonlight in a thick fog. I flipped it, and it grew stronger. "Is this an opal?"

"Moonstone. Can you see the adularescence? The glow or inner light?"

"Yes, it's really pretty." I extended it to her.

She shook her head. "No, hold on to it. I mean that literally. I want you to hold it as much as you can tonight. Do you give your word?"

"Um…" I looked at the gigantic stone then back at her.

"Consider it part of the job." She got up from her seat, the cat leaping to the ground.

"Okay, then yes, I give my word." I squinted and shook my head as my ears started ringing slightly. I worked my jaw, and the sound receded. What a weird day.

"Excuse me a second." She glided out a door on the right side of the room. I hadn't noticed the door initially as it fit perfectly into the wall.

A meow to my left drew my attention to Patagonia, who was pressed into my side and had worked her way under my hand. While yowling in a pleading tone, she pressed her head into the palm of my hand and twisted it back and forth so my nails grazed the fur on the sides. I dutifully scratched behind her ears, digging my nails through her thick fur. She rolled around under my hand to get scratches behind both ears and neck. I didn't trust her after that bite, though she seemed safe now.

I flexed my hand and inspected the wound, or at least where the wound had been. I pulled my hand in close to my face, but where I would expect two large scabs on each side were instead tiny holes that didn't even appear to be open. Patagonia must have needle-thin teeth. I flexed the hand, and though it felt a tiny bit stiff and tingly, it didn't hurt. The skin on my arm was clear. I really needed to ask Olivia what the deal was with all the witnessing stuff and the faint lines. The whole thing had been beyond strange.

I sat up straight. She had not only evaded my questions about the cat bite, faint lines, and all that witnessing business, but then she had distracted me from questions about my father only having a son. Somehow I had ended up looking at a list of numbers and made a promise to hold a rock. Hardly a fair trade. I wanted to know about my father and the cat. And Vin.

I shook my head. I didn't mean Vin. I meant the... I stood up abruptly, and Patagonia meowed her displeasure and caught her claws on my pants. I carefully unhooked her paw and went to the wall Olivia had exited through, but I couldn't find a latch or handle. The edges of the door sat flush against the wall. I headed to the entrance I had entered through, but Patagonia weaved through my feet, tripping me. I fumbled for a few steps then carefully hooked a foot under her belly and gently moved her to my side.

Stepping out the door, I turned to Auntie Ann's desk, but instead of her there was a younger twentysomething with dark hair. "Hello, Miss Gabriella Ramono. How can I help you?"

"I'm looking for Olivia or Ann."

"Hi, I'm Vin's sister, Vanessa. Olivia and Mom left."

Patagonia weaved between my feet, her lithe, solid body vibrating with a purr. "Left?"

"Yes, but they put you on the schedule for tomorrow, and I have everything you need tonight." She picked up a phone, and her voice rose slightly as she spoke. "Can you send up security to help Miss Gabriella to her car?"

"Security!" I said as Patagonia yowled and stood on her back legs to dig her claws into my thigh.

"Security is just to help you get to your car safely and help carry your things." She smiled fondly at Patagonia. Then, startled, she slapped at the knee of her pants where little curls of smoke drifted off the fabric.

Patagonia easily reached my hip without even needing to extend. She seemed bigger than before. Was her coat darker? I adjusted the messenger bag on my shoulder. "I don't need any help. I have just the one bag. I still have a job, right? I should come back tomorrow."

The girl pursed her lips to make a kissy noise while grabbing some nylon straps off her desk. "Come here, Pat the cat. Here, sweetie." Patagonia danced over to her, and she started to put a harness on the cat. "Of course you still have a job. Here." She stood and handed me a leash attached to Patagonia.

Two large men in suits entered, and she gestured to the pile of bags stacked behind the desk.

"Wait, I don't understand. What is all that stuff, and why…?" I lifted the leash in my hand.

"You can't walk Patagonia outside without a leash. It's far too dangerous."

"Outside?" I looked at Patagonia. She looked back then rubbed her head into my knee.

"Of course. How else will you take her home? Don't worry. Everything you need is in the bags, and of course you will bring her to work with you tomorrow. I'm just so excited that she's finally been paired!"

CHAPTER FOUR

After filling my car to the brim with cat supplies and wrestling Patagonia into the front seat, I headed home.

"Don't you dare claw up my car. These seats are real leather." I pulled out onto the Avenue to drive past the glittery casinos before turning down a side road toward a more industrial part of town. It wasn't more than a few minutes off the Avenue, but tourists stayed away, which was smart.

I had expected Patagonia to yowl and hate the car, but instead she meowed with interest and pressed both paws against the window to watch the scenery as we raced by.

The first time I had driven to my dad's building after the lawyer called to tell me of it, I was convinced I would sell it immediately. But once I saw the beautiful loft Dad had called home, I had reconsidered. Then I found out that the tenants, who had been friends of my father, worked on the bottom two floors. Their rent more than covered expenses and left a tidy monthly profit. And despite the industrial area, there was virtually no crime within a two-block neighborhood.

Or at least there were no reported crimes. The bottom floor was an auto salvage company that I suspected dealt

19

with cars obtained through both traditional and more nefarious ways. The security company on the second floor wouldn't tell me all the services they provided, but they were armed to the teeth to do it. Despite that, everyone from the owner to the unpaid interns had been respectful and the owners paid on time.

Patagonia pawed at my shoulder and meowed.

"We're almost home." How I had ended up the owner of a cat was still a mystery to me. Vanessa had been sweet but quite insistent on the arrangement. She had also assured me that Patagonia would never bite me again. In fact, she had found it hilarious that I asked.

I pulled up to the driveway ramp that wrapped up and around the building, allowing me to park my car on the third floor in a garage attached to the loft. I honked as I passed the large rolled-up door of the salvage business, giving a quick wave, and again as I drove by the security firm. It was way past normal businesses' closing time, but it seemed both of them operated at unusual hours.

I pressed the button on the garage and parked inside before closing the door. Patagonia became more agitated, jumping from the front seat to the back and slapping me across the face with her tail.

I opened the back door of the car, where Patagonia leapt free to start exploring the garage.

Fearful she would lick up something she shouldn't off the ground, I opened the door to the loft. "Come inside. I guess you're home."

Patagonia raced past me to explore. Floor-to-vaulted-ceiling windows looked back toward the Avenue. They had some special coating so that you couldn't look in from outside. The open-air design with midcentury modern furniture reminded me of my father. He had liked clean design and everything in its place, but I had had no idea that he had such a nice home of black leather, chrome, and glass.

He must have spent a fortune buying the building

because despite the immense size of the loft, it was easy to keep warm in winter and cool in summer. The walls must have been insulated, or there was a passive ventilation system that I didn't know about.

I pulled out the handwritten notes from Vanessa with directions for the cat. I set out a litter box in the front bathroom and a bowl of food and water in the kitchen.

"Patagonia," I called out before going back into my garage to get the last bag of cat toys and a large cat bed. As I slammed the trunk, a white glint caught my eye in the passenger seat. The moonstone egg must have fallen out of my purse. I had promised to hold it, so I juggled the load and opened the passenger door.

Without any pockets on my slim business suit, I wedged the egg into my cleavage. My super padded add-two-cup-sizes bra guaranteed that egg wasn't going anywhere. I had thought the stone would be cool, but instead it was warm to the touch.

I bumped the door shut with my hip and went inside, closing the door to the garage. "Patagonia. Your food's here."

I kicked off my shoes and set out the cat bed. "Patagonia? Where did you go?" I blew out a breath. "Pat!" I heard a meow from overhead. Looking up, I spotted Patagonia walking across an exposed roof support beam. "Get down from there."

She effortlessly leaped from the beam to the top of a bookcase then soared through the air to land silently on the couch next to me.

I gasped. "Don't do that."

She looked at me and blinked slowly before jumping off the couch to sniff at her food bowl. She reached out to take a bite then batted at the bowl. It went sliding across the floor, slammed into the refrigerator, and sprayed little crunchy kitty kibble everywhere.

I sighed and started to get up to sweep up the mess before my robotic vacuum that used to be my only companion got clogged on the mess, but something caught my eye. The small chest that my father had left me was sitting on the coffee table, and it really looked as if there was a light coming from inside.

Everything my father had was left to me in his will, not that any of it was worth losing him. But the simple wooden chest was the only thing mentioned in the will as something he specifically wanted me to have. It was actually a stipulation of the will that I always keep it even if I sold everything else. When the lawyer gave it to me, I knew I would never have gotten rid of it even if the will were different. The inside smelled of my father's cologne, a woody scent that brought back memories of all the time we had spent together. The interior was packed full of photographs of the two of us from our vacations all over the world. I could barely stand to look at them because my grief tore a hole in my chest. Maybe one day.

I picked up the pile of photos and set them on the table carefully. The top picture was of me in Italy, pretending to hold up the leaning tower of Pisa. I wiped away a tear. Lifting the chest into my lap, I examined the bottom of the chest. Where the bottom met the sides, there was a thin line of light radiating up on all four sides.

In the center of the bottom was a round divot the size of a quarter. The light slowly turned purple. I wiped my brow and realized I was hot. A trickle of sweat rolled down my chest, and as I wiped it away, I brushed against the stone egg, which was toasty to the touch. When I pulled it out, the stone glowed with a hazy purple light.

I looked back at the box with the round divot in the middle. Patagonia came over to sit next to me. I reached over and scratched behind her ears. "I'm no genius, but I think my next step is obvious."

I took the egg and set it in the box, spinning it until it settled into the divot perfectly. The egg and light glowed then went out with an audible click. I lifted the egg and tucked it back into my cleavage then tipped the chest so the false bottom shifted and fell into my hand.

Inside were a short handwritten note in my father's distinctive script and a necklace with a large peach translucent stone the size of a quarter. The stone was surrounded by diamonds, and the necklace was quite heavy as I picked it up.

I read the note out loud.

"Dear Ella,

Never forget how much I love you. I never want you to have to follow in my footsteps, but if you do and I can't be there to guide you, then I know that Bear and Badger will train you well. They are my closest friends, and you can trust them. At this point in your studies, you will need this necklace. Wear it and know I am near.

Love, Dad."

I stared at the note and reread it then flipped it over, but nothing was on the back. "That makes no sense."

I didn't know anyone named Bear or Badger, and I had never heard Dad speak of them. There was so much that I didn't know about his life. I regretted deeply that I hadn't asked more questions about his life. I didn't even have the excuse that I was young, as he passed when I was in my midtwenties, old enough to know better, but after college I was always so busy at my job.

What did he mean about following in his footsteps? I had planned to research the casino after my weird day, but none of that mattered now. I put on the necklace and carefully put everything back in the chest. I needed to know who my dad was and what he did. I stood up and headed for my bathroom. I would shower, then I would see what I could find on the internet and in my father's papers.

CHAPTER FIVE

When I woke up on the couch the next morning, there was a heavy weight on my chest and an unfamiliar chiming filling the air. I struggled to push Patagonia off my chest, but she dug her claws through the fabric of my thick robe and yowled her displeasure.

"Off!" I used a firm voice that the internet assured me would tell an animal that I was the boss.

She glared at me while the chiming continued then slowly rose and turned her backside to my face before jumping to the coffee table. She meowed once, kicked my notebook onto the floor, knocked over a cup filled with colored pens, then glared at me. After sighing in disgust, she winked, jumped to the floor, and slowly padded off.

I rubbed my eyes. I had fallen asleep at the crack of dawn after spending all night trying to figure out what my father's note had meant and who Bear and Badger were. I had discovered nothing.

The chimes started again, sounding like church bells, then my cell phone started ringing as well. The name of the security firm on the second floor was on the screen.

"Hello?" I croaked into the phone.

"Sorry to bother you, Ella. This is Lou Freeman of

Freeman Security. I saw a car drive up to your place and wanted to make sure you were okay."

"Oh, the doorbell," I muttered into the phone. That explained the chimes. No one had ever visited other than the tenants from downstairs who called before they headed up and I met in the garage to let them in. I hadn't heard the doorbell before.

"I ran the plate, and it belongs to Vin Russo. If you would like, I can come up with some of my men."

Vin was here? "No, I think it's fine. I took a job at the Golden Pyramid casino yesterday, and I guess I overslept." I wandered over to the coffee maker and pressed Start.

"And they sent over Vin to wake you up?" The doubt was heavy in his voice, and I couldn't blame him. It didn't make sense to me either.

"It's okay. Thank you so much for calling and checking on me, but I'm fine."

The line was quiet for several beats before he replied. "Keep your emergency signal in hand, and I would like to come over soon to talk to you."

"I have it in my hand right now. I'll be in touch soon." I clicked off the line. He was a good tenant, and part of his rent was paid in the most up-to-date security measures on the planet. I grabbed my keys with the emergency button on them.

The chimes went off again, and I slowly padded to the front door. I couldn't imagine how much of a train wreck I looked like, but I took the time to grab my butt-length red hair and twist it into a bun before unlocking the door—a process of turning over the heavy bolts and pressing a shoulder to the door to relieve some pressure before it creaked open.

Vin stood at the threshold, radiating intense anger. His face was red and his hands in fists. "I've been standing out here for ten minutes."

I stared at him then gave a leisurely yawn. "And you can stay there the rest of the day if you act like that. What

25

are you doing here?"

I turned around and strode back toward the kitchen to get coffee, partially to cover my morning breath but mostly to wake me up for this conversation.

"You said you would be in this morning at nine a.m. Olivia sent me over when you didn't show up or answer your phone."

I hoped he didn't see my flinch at his reply. His anger was evident, but despite Lou's concern, I didn't feel unsafe. In fact, I was feeling sassy and bold. "You can come in for a cup of coffee and explain why they would send you over for a mere accountant." I aimed for bored and casual and hoped he didn't detect the hesitation in my voice.

"I'll take some coffee." He shut the door and followed me into the kitchen. "Nice place. Does it normally look like it's been hit by a tornado?"

I looked around at the destruction from my late-night search. Books and journals had been pulled down from all the bookshelves. The file cabinet was still open, and there was a stack of folders on the desk. The cat food was still dotting the floor along with the pens and notebook that Patagonia batted around this morning. "I was looking for something."

Patagonia jumped on the counter, and before I could yell at her, she shoved one of the coffee mugs off the edge. It shattered into a thousand pieces, then she ran and disappeared.

I gasped and grabbed a broom to sweep up.

"Sure." He followed me to the counter where the coffee maker was. "This is a nice place, but what did your dad have against walls?"

I chuckled and got down a new mug. "It's a loft. It's not supposed to have walls. It is all one great room. Except the bathrooms. Obviously."

"What about the bedroom?" He had his back to me as he spun slowly to take it all in.

A chill passed through me at his mention of the bedroom, and surprisingly, it wasn't altogether unpleasant. "It's tucked into a back corner, and there are barn doors that you can roll shut to keep the temperature more comfortable. It's kind of its own room, I suppose." I busied myself getting out the sugar cubes from the cabinet and heavy whipping cream from the refrigerator. No mere half-and-half for me.

Vin came over and reached around me to grab a mug. The heat radiating off him made me painfully aware that I was in my pajamas under my robe.

I stretched my neck and spotted my cat on top of the cabinets, eyeing Vin. Before I could say anything, she leapt smoothly across the dozen feet to land on his shoulder then bound to the floor.

Vin didn't even flinch. "I see Patagonia is settling in."

That raised a whole mess of questions that I had been pondering all night between searching for clues from my father. "Why did Olivia give me Patagonia? And what was the deal yesterday with the whole 'witnessed by one' business?" I took a sip of the piping-hot coffee, it fueling my curiosity. "And the sheet with the numbers? And no one really explained the thing about thinking my dad only had a son."

"If you had come in today, you could've asked Olivia all that yourself." He gave me a smug smile.

I shook my head. "I kinda have some other things to figure out first."

"You're coming. Now." His voice carried a weight that made me want to give in.

I took a step toward the bathroom before Patagonia twined between my feet and sent me tumbling to the floor. My mug hit the floor and shattered. Coffee sprayed out around me and soaked into the robe. The couch was between us, so while Vin had seen me fall, he couldn't see the hot tears that started to spill. That mug had been one of my father's. I wiped them off my face and stood up.

Hot rage drove out any embarrassment. I jabbed a finger in his direction. "You don't tell me what to do. No one does."

"You work for the casino."

"Then I quit. The casino hired me to be an accountant. I don't want to get mixed up in your weird family voodoo stuff." I whipped off my coffee-covered robe and examined the red silk pants and chemise I had underneath.

Vin's eyes darted down then quickly back to my face. "Let me start over. Olivia would like you to come. She said that she has a lot of answers for you."

That was something that interested me. "Answers?"

"Yes. Why don't you change and I'll drive you over. They're waiting for you. They've been calling for hours."

"Before I go to sleep, I set my phone to only allow calls through from certain numbers. I have insomnia." I looked down at the coffee and mug shards.

"Get ready, and I'll even clean up your mess. Where's a mop?"

I could get my answers then come home. "Deal. The farthest right cabinet in the kitchen." Then I went to my bedroom to get ready.

A quick wash of my face, running a brush through my hair then pinning it up, and a clean change of clothing were pretty much all I needed. After brushing my teeth, I dropped my sopping-wet robe and pajamas into the washer, where they clanged against the metal drum.

Fishing around in there, I pulled out the moonstone egg that had been in the robe pocket. I attempted to jam it into my jeans pocket, but when it stuck out awkwardly and dug into my hipbone, I wedged it into my cleavage again and buttoned up my shirt to hide it. Then I adjusted the necklace I had found last night.

I found Vin and Patagonia sitting on the couch, enjoying a cup of coffee together. The loft was much cleaner. Not only had he cleaned up the coffee and mug, but he must have swept up the cat food, picked up the pens and notebook, then arranged the rest of the files and books in neat piles. A prickly feeling of unease made me wonder if he didn't also take a quick glance through them as he helpfully cleaned up.

"Thank you for cleaning. If you ever need some extra cash, I could hire you as a cleaner." I grabbed my purse off the counter.

"You can't afford me. Make sure to grab Patagonia and your channeling key."

I turned to face him. "I'm not bringing Patagonia, and what's a channeling key?"

"Fine, don't bring Patagonia. And I mean that moonstone egg. You have been carrying it with you, haven't you?" He sneered a bit and sounded just like a disapproving teacher.

I smirked and pushed out my chest. I stared him right in the eyes and hooked my index finger into the top of my shirt, pulling the fabric down until I revealed my bra-enhanced cleavage and the egg nestled in between my breasts. I wanted it to look sexy and intimidating. "Good enough?"

Vin and the cat burst out laughing. "You look like you're trying to hatch an egg, but I guess that'll work."

My cheeks heated, and I knew I didn't want to be trapped at the casino without a car. "Let me just grab one last thing, and I'll be ready to go."

I raced into the garage and started my car. As I backed out of the garage, Vin came storming out after me before running to his car and following me down the driveway. At the bottom of the driveway, Mike Clinton, the owner of Clinton Automotive, stepped out and flagged me down.

I rolled down my passenger window and leaned over. "Hi, Mike."

"Hi, Ella. Say, I think it's time for you to bring your car over for an oil change."

"Thanks, Mike, but not today." I checked my rearview mirror and saw his employees were pushing a car across the driveway, blocking Vin from following me.

Vin laid on the horn.

Mike casually looked at Vin then back at me. "Your friend is awfully impatient."

"He's no friend, just a work acquaintance. You can take your time with that car. He'll be fine waiting a bit."

Mike gave a little chuckle. "Understood. I'm serious about your car. You need to bring it over within a week. Putting off car maintenance is dangerous."

"Deal." I checked the rearview mirror. Vin was getting out of his car. "And thanks for dealing with him. I just need a head start." I rolled up the window and couldn't resist peeling out of the driveway.

CHAPTER SIX

When I strode into the Golden Pyramid casino, I found myself checking over my shoulder for Vin. He was going to be hopping mad when he arrived. I stopped in front of a life-size replica of the Sphinx—though this version housed a bar—to figure out where I should go. If I went left, I could go to the accounting department, as I had yesterday, and ask my boss what to do, or I could go right to security and ask them to call upstairs to Olivia.

I knew they were expecting me, but I wasn't sure *where* they expected me. I was confused, unsure, and had no idea why I was here. Maybe this was why Vin was so determined that I drive with him.

"Miss Ramono?"

I turned around, and a tall man stood behind me. He was in a suit and could pass for a businessman if not for the earpiece that all security staff wore on duty.

"Yes. I'm supposed to meet with Olivia Santini." I threw back my shoulders and tried to give off an air of confidence.

"She's waiting for you." He turned and walked off.

I assumed I was supposed to follow him and struggled to keep up without jogging as his long legs ate up the distance ahead of him. His people skills could use some work.

Eventually, he stopped in front of the elevators and pressed the call button. One instantly opened. He stepped in and pressed a button then held the door.

After I stepped inside, he lowered his hand and stepped out. "Ms. Santini will meet you there."

The elevator door closed and started up as I mentally rehearsed my questions. I wanted to know why they gave me a cat and what the deal was with the cat bite. And why she gave me the stone. What had Vin called it? A channeling something. How had it opened that box my dad left me? Maybe it was magnetic or electronic. I hadn't looked at that sheet of numbers she had given me, but she needed to be honest about what was going on first.

I blew out a breath. Too many thoughts and questions were bouncing around my head. I would never remember them all. What was the most important question? I would start there. What did they know about my father? That was the most vital thing. What had they heard about him, what did he do when he worked here, and did they know anything about why he was killed. The cat, stone, numbers, and such could wait.

The elevator opened, and I hesitantly stepped out onto a floor that was under construction. Tools were stacked in a pile, and exposed wooden beams formed the skeleton of rooms.

"There you are, Ella. Where's Vin? Where's Patagonia?" Olivia waved me over to where she stood next to Auntie Ann.

Light filtered in through the windows, which were covered in thick plastic. I carefully picked my way through the mess. "What are we doing here?"

"Glad you asked. Watch this." Olivia flipped open a tablet, pressed a few buttons, then turned it toward me.

A video started playing on the screen. It was shot from a high angle, probably by a security camera, and was of this floor unless there was another floor under construction with the exact same hammers and tool belt in the exact same pile. A few seconds into the footage, a middle-aged couple exited the same elevator I had just left. There was no sound, but it appeared that in the dim light of nighttime, they spoke to each other, then the woman turned toward a window and raced over to it. She then stepped out. The man ran after her, looked out the window, then collapsed on the floor. On that, the video ended.

"What you do think?" Olivia looked at me expectantly.

I was shaking slightly. I felt as if snippets of the video were familiar, but I couldn't remember ever seeing it. "She jumped?"

Olivia nodded. "Yes, she's the suicide you mentioned yesterday. What do you think happened?"

"Why are you asking me? That's awful. That poor woman." A brush of fur rubbed against my leg, and I jumped.

Patagonia meowed and rubbed against me again.

Olivia looked over my shoulder. "Glad you could join us, Vinny."

I couldn't see him yet, but I could feel his presence behind me. Cold prickles moved across the back of my neck, and I fought against my urge to turn and look at him.

"I ran into a little holdup." He came to my side and glowered at me.

I turned and tried to plaster a nonchalant smile on my face. "Oh, you made it, and you brought Patagonia."

He narrowed his eyes. "I didn't. You did."

I opened my mouth to question him, but Olivia interrupted.

"Please, Ella, focus. What happened?" Olivia gestured at her tablet.

"Olivia." Auntie Ann placed her hand on Olivia's arm. "We need to tell her about her ability first. She doesn't understand."

I looked between them. "Tell me what?"

Auntie Ann turned to me. "Honey, your father had a special ability. He could tell people's motives, what their character was, what they were feeling, that kind of thing. That's a hereditary ability, and you inherited it."

"Like psychic? No, no, he was always good at reading people and predicting their behavior, but that's just being observant. He taught me how to do a lot of that, but it wasn't something I inherited."

Olivia stepped in front of her aunt. "It's a special ability. A magical ability. He was a mage. You're a mage. We're all mages. And you have your father's ability to know things about people. Now tell me what you know." She shoved the tablet at me.

Auntie Ann pulled Olivia back with a shushing noise. "Sweetie, calm down. You should have slept last night. Give her some time to understand." She looked at Vin and cut her eyes over to me.

Vin sighed. "I know it is a lot to take in." Anger still tinged his voice.

Questions bounced around in my head. Not the least of which was if I was alone with a bunch of lunatics. "Mage? Like a magician? Like abracadabra?"

Vin rolled his eyes. "Not the kind of magician that pulls a rabbit out of a hat or a fairytale. Mage or witch or magic practitioner. What term you prefer. You inherit the ability to work magic from either parent, and when a parent dies, their children inherit additional abilities. It used to be just the oldest son, but times change, and now we realize that if parents spent time and loved their children, it would go to all of them. For whatever reason, your father didn't want us or the rest of the community to know about you. That's why he always said he only had a son."

"This…" It was unbelievable what he was saying, except for the weird note last night. And the fact that Dad did seem to always know about people's character better than anyone else should have ever known. When we had traveled, he had spotted every conman, pickpocket, or other undesirable. But this was too much to believe. "I think you have me confused with someone. I'll just go."

Olivia grabbed my arm as I turned to leave. "Tell us about the fire."

I shivered and slowly turned around. "You read about it on the internet, didn't you?"

She nodded. "Do you still have nightmares?"

I broke out in a cold sweat as a wave of nausea passed briefly over me. "Yes. That's when I started having problems sleeping."

"Tell us about it." Vin's voice had lost its anger. Even with his rough, rumbly voice, it was almost gentle.

"One of my coworkers tried to shoot me at the office, but there was a fluke fire, and he died instead." It sounded so mild in comparison to what happened.

Vin stepped fully in front of me so he was the only one I could see. "Your coworker had been embezzling, right? And you knew?"

I frowned. "Frank was such a snake. I knew he was up to something."

"And your boss didn't believe you, did he?"

"No! No one believed me. I never had a good feeling about Frank from the moment he moved to our office, but then I started to think it was more than just him being a douche. He was crooked."

"That was right after your dad passed, wasn't it?"

I looked at Vin in surprise. I had taken several weeks off to handle Dad's affairs. "You're right. I returned to work, and Frank was handling one of my accounts. Something was off."

"How did you know? We called your old boss, and he said that Frank's plan had been perfect and to this day he doesn't know how you spotted it. In fact, he seemed a bit suspicious." Vin arched an eyebrow at me.

Frustration welled up in me. "Frank was so slimy. The way he said stuff, how he acted, even how he handled work showed he was crooked."

Vin leaned in a little. "Tell me how."

All my frustration erupted. "I just knew! I *knew*." My mouth was running away from me. Even all these years later, I was still furious that no one had believed me, and it almost cost me my life. I was practically screaming. "He was a crook, and I knew it from the second I saw him. And I was right. I *told* them he was up to something, but no one believed me, then someone said something to him. *They* didn't believe me, but Frank knew I was right, and he came after me with a gun! He waited until I was working late and snuck in. He was going to shoot me—" With a gasp, I cut myself off. Tears started rolling down my face.

Auntie Ann stepped around Vin. "It's okay. You can tell us."

I choked back a sob. "He had the gun pointed right at me, then... then there was fire everywhere. He was engulfed in flames and screaming. The screaming was awful." I dabbed at my eyes. "Frank died, and the office building was mostly destroyed. I told the police that he had pulled a gun, and all of Frank's lies quickly unraveled. They ended up giving me quite a severance package so I wouldn't sue."

Auntie Ann handed me a tissue. "You did the right thing. He would have killed you."

"I didn't... What do you mean?" I looked between Auntie Ann and Vin.

"Sweetheart." She kept her voice calm and gentle. "You started the fire the same way you knew he was a criminal. It is part of being a mage."

Vin nodded. "Creating fire spontaneously is a sign of a mage that doesn't have a handle on their abilities."

The idea that I had burned a man to death was too much. "I never would have done that."

"Shhh." Auntie Ann stroked my shoulder. "It wasn't on purpose. You don't have training. The only way you could have produced that much magic was because you feared for your life."

It was so much to take in. I dreamed of the fire often, the flames licking across my skin but not burning me. The firemen that had arrived said it was a miracle that I had made it out alive. My clothes had burned, but my hair didn't even smell of smoke.

"I don't understand." I had a million questions in my head that all fought to get out at once, but I remembered my resolution in the elevator. "Tell me about my dad."

Olivia hopped in front of Vin and Auntie Ann. "We will. That's part of the deal. You help us, and we'll help you. Now it's your turn." She extended the tablet.

"I don't know what I'm doing. Can't you get a mage that knows what they're doing to help you?"

Vin snorted. "Why didn't we think of that? There are plenty of them just sitting around everywhere." His voice was heavy with sarcasm.

I glared at him. "How about a little less attitude, especially when you're asking me for help."

"Dear, your type of ability isn't particularly common, and we don't even know if you can read an emotional hologram. When there are strong emotions combined with magic, they get imprinted on the location, at least for a time. Mages like your family who can read emotions of people usually can read emotional holograms as well."

"So you can't do it?" I looked between the three of them.

Vin's face turned slightly red. "Our family has different abilities." He bit off the words. "Useful ones."

"Vincent!" Auntie Ann snapped then dragged him over to the elevator. She lowered her voice, but it carried back to us. "I don't know what has gotten into you. You are acting below your station."

The muscles in his jaw flexed. "You're coddling her. You should—"

"Do *not* speak to me in that tone." She was no longer a soft motherly figure. Instead, she radiated cold power.

Vin fought with himself but eventually said, "Why don't I go downstairs and help Vanessa gather up the information?"

"Thank you, Vincent." Auntie Ann took a deep breath while Vin got into the elevator before she returned. "Ella, are you ready to try this?"

My head was spinning. "I'm not sure if…" Could Dad's note from last night have to do with being a mage? "I think I need to go home." I felt overwhelmed until Patagonia rubbed up against my leg.

Patagonia stood on her back legs and, with a mighty leap, jumped at my chest. I wrapped my arms around her furry body as she dug her claws into my belly and pushed her head against my face. Her soft fur pressed into my neck soothed me. The gentle purring emanating from her gave me a warm, fuzzy feeling all over. I felt loved and supported, though I struggled under her weight until she jumped down.

Olivia sighed. "You need to help us. The ides is only a few days away, and someone else will die."

"*What?*"

"You noticed the pattern on the ides of each month, and we spent all yesterday researching, and the dates lined up with suicides or accidental deaths that have occurred at the casino and payouts we gave to the surviving family. Dad must have noticed or felt that something was off. We went back five months and found the pattern. There is clearly something happening, but we don't know what or how."

Before I could reply, Auntie Ann spoke. "We don't expect you to solve this alone. We just need a direction to look. Olivia didn't even know what the numbers on her father's desk meant until you gave us a pattern to look for, then we found it. That is all we are asking, to give us a direction to look toward. And we will give you something in return. We can help you learn about your gifts and how to use them. Plus, we can tell you about your father."

"What can you tell me?" I leaned forward in anticipation. This was what I wanted.

Olivia shook a finger. "No, you help us solve the deaths first, then we will help you."

"My father was murdered. If you have information—"

Tears welled up in Olivia's eyes. "You're not the only one who lost a father. My father had information about this situation on his desk when he was found. Maybe it is unconnected to his murder, but if it is…"

"Murder? I thought your father took his own life."

"That is what the police thought because there was no evidence of another person, but we think it was another mage, someone who could use magic to hide their tracks." She looked away and quickly ran a hand across her eyes.

She might be the CEO of the largest and best casino in Rambler, but she was also a daughter missing her father. That was something I could relate to. "I understand. And if I do my best to help you, then you will give me information about my father? You promise? I'm not convinced I can do what you think I can do, but if I try, that's enough?"

She nodded. "Yes, we can tell you what we know about him, and right now I have a secretary pulling information together on all the situations your father helped with at the casino. I am sure you will find a lot of information in there."

I would prefer to get all the information first, but this seemed like a fair deal. "Okay, I agree. I will do my best to help you, and you will give me the information I want. What do I do?"

Olivia shoved the tablet at me. "Perfect. Watch this."

"Hold up, Olivia." Auntie Ann took the tablet from Olivia's hand. "First, let me help Ella." She turned to me. "Do you have your channeling key on you? That's the stone egg Olivia gave you."

"Yes." I turned away and grabbed it from my cleavage then held it out in my hand.

Auntie Ann chuckled. "Good. Keep that on you. It collects spare energy from you, then you can use it later when you need it. And keep Patagonia with you. She will help you as well."

"Patagonia? What do you—"

Olivia snorted. "We'll explain later."

Auntie Ann raised an eyebrow at Olivia then turned back to me. "Yes, we will get to all this later. You have a lot to learn. Close your eyes, and try to push away all your questions for now. Take a deep, slow breath in, hold it, then let it out."

I did what she asked, including pushing away the questions that were assaulting my mind. I struggled until Patagonia pressed up against my leg, then I felt everything but that exact moment in time fading away.

"Good. Now watch the video and observe. Don't try too hard. Just watch, and whatever you observe, say out loud. The fact that we are here, where it happened, should help you."

I opened my eyes and felt strangely confident. Memories of travelling with my father flooded my head. No matter where we were, even if we didn't speak the language, we played the same game. We would sit on a bench and people watch. He would point out body language such as how close or far people stood, how they looked at each other or orientated their feet and body toward another person, and make guesses as to who they were, how they felt about each other, and such. Dad would point out little things until I felt I practically knew these people and who they were.

Perhaps he had been training me to use my gift even then. Those observation skills had served me well through school and in my job. I had always been good at unraveling puzzles involving people, and it was part of what drove me into auditing. I had considered forensic accounting, but the state auditors of Nevada had a surprisingly fun department and recruiting program. I had been good at my job, especially when I went on-site to observe the department I was auditing. What Olivia and Auntie Ann told me made sense in light of my skill set.

I took the tablet, and the video started to play. I watched the man and woman interact and paused the video. "They were disagreeing about something. Look at how she whips around when he talks. She's annoyed with him for what he said."

"Good, dear." Auntie Ann nodded with approval. "Now go stand where they stood and just quietly stand there and tell me if you feel anything."

I walked over ten feet to the entrance of the elevator and rewatched the start of the video. Emotions started to tickle the back of my mind. They felt real but weren't connected to me. "She was already annoyed with him when they arrived. Then he said something, and…"

I played the video. The woman was snapping at him when suddenly her face changed and her head whipped toward the window that was covered with plastic. I walked over to that spot and closed my eyes. "Something scared her… no, surprised her. It surprised her, then…"

Olivia was watching me and nodding.

Auntie Ann smiled. "You're doing great. Just relax and let it come to you."

I watched the video a few times to the end then walked to the window. Emotions rolled over me. A great loss that brought tears to my eyes and at the same time, incredible joy. The sensation of recovery of someone. I let the tears flow down my face for a bit and let the feeling of reuniting fill me. "She heard something from this window. It was a person she desperately wanted to see. She didn't jump to her death. She… I don't know how to say this. I guess she felt she was going toward someone out there. See how she is reaching out?" I flipped the tablet to show Auntie Ann and Olivia, who had followed me as I moved around the floor. "She was reaching out to someone who was there. Or she thought was there?"

Auntie Ann smiled. "Do you feel love?"

I closed my eyes, and there it was. Love. "Yes."

"Then it was real. A lot of emotions can be faked with magic but not real genuine love. If she was drawn by love, then whoever it was really existed in some form."

I closed my eyes again and swayed slightly. Nothing else came to me. "I think that's it."

"You did wonderfully. You will need to eat, and we can talk more. Olivia, call down and arrange for us to take a private dining room. We'll eat and talk about what to do next."

Olivia pulled out her phone. "Which restaurant?"

Auntie Ann gasped. "There is only one thing to eat after big magic. Italian, of course!"

CHAPTER SEVEN

I dragged a half of a pumpkin ravioli through the sauce and stuffed it into my mouth. As I chewed, I leaned back in the chair and moaned. "This is amazing!"

Auntie Ann passed over a plate of stuffed mushrooms. "The food here is excellent, but it is also because you just performed magic. Nothing whets the appetite like a good magical workout."

We were in a private room at the casino's nicest restaurant, Isadora's Ristorante. Vin and Vanessa had joined us to eat. In addition to the food that kept appearing, red wine filled all our glasses. The conversation had been sparse as we dug into our meal.

"If I keep doing magic and eating like this, I'm going to be too big to fit through the doorway." I spooned more food onto my plate and drained my wine glass.

She chuckled. "It also burns up a lot of calories. Nothing is without a cost."

I thanked the server who refilled my wine glass. I had a pleasant buzz but was nowhere near drunk despite starting on my third glass. In fact, I felt great all over—strong, energized, and emotionally buoyant. I was tired but less weary. It felt more like the fatigue after a great workout.

The serving staff left as a beautiful older lady pushed in a cart. She had a white streak in her black hair and a lineless face that made me question my initial impression of her age.

"I've brought in the dessert tray. It has samples of everything but the chocolate cakes. You know those are special order. What are we celebrating?" She looked around the room with a sweet expression on her face, her eyes pausing on Patagonia perched in a chair and eating chicken off a plate.

Auntie Ann reached out and patted the woman's arm. "Everything is just wonderful, Isadora. I don't think anyone has your gift with food."

Olivia got up and inspected the dessert cart. "Please tell Beth that these all look wonderful. And don't worry about the cat hair on the chair. I've already put in an order to housekeeping. We won't be needing anything more today. Thank you."

Isadora bowed her head. "Enjoy your meal." She exited.

Vanessa started to talk, but Olivia held up a hand for her to stop then went over to the door and firmly shut it. "Nothing we say is to leave this room."

Vin got up and grabbed a zeppole. The powdered sugar sifted over it glistened and shone like newly fallen snowflakes. "Are we ready to get to work?"

Olivia rolled her eyes at him then took an empty seat at the table and started pulling out notebooks. "The ides of this month is in two days, so that gives us just about forty-eight hours to prevent the next suicide. Though I am gathering information from various departments, no one else except us is to know about the deaths or anything regarding our investigation. Ella, can you get out your channel key? The stone egg."

I swallowed the fettuccini Alfredo I was eating and reached into my pocket to display the egg in the palm of me hand.

"Great. Can you repeat after me? I promise to speak to only the people in this room about the investigation."

"I promise to speak to only the people in this room about the investigation." I felt a brief tightening in my chest that released a second later. "Oh, weird." I raised an eyebrow at Olivia.

"Just a magical binding. You won't be able to do anything that you believe breaks your promise. Now let's dig into—"

"Hold up. What is the channel key exactly? If you want me to help, it's only fair that you explain some things."

"We really need to get started, and I already explained that it stores up extra magic."

I thought about the egg opening the secret compartment in the chest last night. "Why is it called a key? Does it open locks?"

Olivia raised her eyebrows in surprise and looked at Auntie Ann.

She beamed at me. Behind her, a plate of cheesecake rose in the air and wobbled toward Vanessa. "Excellent question, dear. Yes, it does, though that is one of its more esoteric uses. It was often used in the past to secure information so that only another magic user could access the information in the safe, but nowadays, email is just as effective most times. We can discuss it more after the investigation."

"We can?"

"Of course. We aren't just going to dump you. You need training."

Vanessa sneezed, and the levitating plate of cheesecake burst into flames and dropped into the center of the table.

Vin snorted and flicked a hand. A large water pitcher next to the tiny inferno tipped over and, with a loud sizzle, extinguished the growing wildfire. Patagonia hissed as water spilled on her face. She glared at Vin, grabbed the remaining chicken from the plate, and curled up in the seat to finish her meal.

Auntie Ann grabbed another plate of cheesecake for Vanessa as she narrowed her eyes at her children. "Cut it out, both of you. You're making a huge mess. We're trying to discuss Ella's training."

Olivia tapped a pen on her notebook. "We haven't agreed to that yet. We have to see how this works out."

Auntie Ann pursed her lips. "When we witnessed her bonding, we agreed to mentor her. You as well, Vincent."

He held up both hands. "No way. I told Olivia that I wanted nothing to do with *her.*" He cut his eyes over to me.

She waggled her finger at her son. "You know that is not how it works."

Seeing the opportunity to get another question answered, I interrupted. "Bonding? Is that what happened when Patagonia bit me? What was the deal with all the lines on my arm?"

Auntie Ann turned to me, and her voice fell into the rhythm I remember from my school days when a teacher would recite a long-known lesson. "Patagonia is a special magical cat, and when they have found the right mage, they bite you to create a bond, but it must be witnessed in order to finish. It is usually done in a formal setting after training, much like graduation."

Vin grumbled under his breath. "Yeah, when you're like eighteen."

She continued as though he hadn't spoken. "Patagonia will help you to perform magic beyond your current strength level, but don't believe for a second that you own her. She can come and go as she pleases and will let you know if something displeases her."

Vanessa finished off her cake and swallowed hard. "She's like your fuzzy magical sidekick."

I stood, grabbed a zeppole off the tray, and bit into it. My eyebrows shot up in shock. Though the little doughy dessert had been sitting out for a while, the chocolatey center was quite warm. In contrast, the white powder on the outside was sweet like sugar but ice cold. The competing temperatures sent a chill over my body followed by cozy warmth that reminded me of sitting by the fire on a snowy night.

I bit into the outside and shivered then nibbled the gooey center to warm up. I stared at the dessert, contemplating how it was cooked so that the outside was cold and the inside was hot.

Sensing my confusion, Vanessa said, "The zeppoles are magic. Duh."

"Oh," I said lamely. After seeing a floating cheesecake, I should have made the leap in logic quicker. I stuffed the rest of the dessert in my mouth then got back to the conversation at hand. "What do you mean Patagonia comes and goes as she pleases?" I reached over and ran a hand over Patagonia's head and scratched behind her ears.

Patagonia meowed loudly and put a paw on her plate, pushing down on one side and letting go so it clanked on the table. I scooped up some chicken and slid it onto her plate.

Auntie Ann poured cream into her coffee and stirred. "Just what I said. She doesn't need to be next to you to assist you, but it helps. Plus, some familiars prefer to be with you. If you leave her at home, like you did today, and she wants to be with you, then she will."

"What? I thought Vin brought her."

He shook his head.

She took a sip of her coffee before continuing. "Nope, she came because she wanted to be with you. Maybe she knew you needed her, or she is just eager to be around you after waiting for almost a decade."

I gasped. "She's already ten years old?"

"Don't worry. She will likely live as long as you do."

Olivia walked around the table and passed out notebooks. "I think she's had enough lesson time for now. We really need to focus, unless everyone is cool with people dying?"

"No need to be dramatic, dear. We are all here to help. " Auntie Ann took a sip from her coffee cup then winced. Looking around the table, she spotted the little bowl with sugar cubes. Two little white squares rose from the bowl and shot across the table to land in her cup.

"Thank you, Auntie. Let me catch up everyone on what I know." Olivia flipped open a folder. "My investigation started when I found the sheet of dates and numbers on Dad's desk after he died. It was not a standard report from the accounting department, and I know that he was working on something before he was killed. I thought maybe it was about embezzling or theft, so I was hesitant to talk to anyone in the accounting department. That's why I brought Ella on board to do an audit of the casino. I had no idea of her relation to Ramono the Bull or her magic ability. Talk about a lucky break."

Auntie Ann interrupted. "No such thing as luck when magic is involved."

Behind her, a zeppole floated off the tray and danced toward Vanessa. Each jerk and bounce sent a gentle snowfall of powdered sugar drifting off the pastry. Vanessa extended a hand to pluck it from the air, when a sugar cube zoomed up underneath it and smacked it off its path. I blinked at the suddenness and looked around for the missing zeppole. With a splat, it hit me between the eyes, and everything around me disappeared in a cold poof of white.

Vin snickered while Vanessa gasped in shock. Patagonia stood on my chest and licked some of the sugar off me.

Olivia rolled her eyes. "Anyways, once Ella noticed the pattern of the dates being on the ides and it corresponding with the sum of fifty thousand dollars, I had a place to start. Fifty thousand dollars is the standard payment the casino gives to people's family when there is a death at the casino, regardless if the casino is at fault or not."

I reached for a napkin. "Does that happen a lot?"

"No, not really, but people drink too much, some try drugs. Occasionally, there are heart attacks or strokes, and rarely there are suicides or accidents, but they do happen. Those are the rarest since we invest a lot of magic and energy into making the casino a happy place. People are more likely to spend money. Ella not only noticed the sum of fifty thousand, but remembered that a lady had committed suicide on one of the ides. That's when I made the connection between the suspicious deaths and the date."

"Are the ides a significant date? Like a magical date?" I was writing down notes.

"Not that I know of, but it probably has significance to the person casting the spell. Maybe they are a big fan of Julius Caesar or Shakespeare. A good spell uses information that is significant to the caster. Patterns are also very powerful."

"So you're sure that a mage is behind the suicides?"

"Yes. The fact that you found a magical imprint at the site of Ethel's suicide was enough to convince me, but I was pretty sure of it before that because of the pattern. A series of murders can be done without magic, but causing someone to kill themselves? Definitely magic. Now, once I knew what the payments were for and the dates, I was able to go to the right department and get the names of the victims. And this is why I didn't tell Isadora what we are doing, and neither will you. The first victim was her son."

Auntie Ann gasped. "No! I remember when Michael overdosed in the parking lot. He had so many problems with drugs that it never occurred to me that something nefarious had happened. Isadora was heartbroken."

Olivia nodded. "I'm not sure if she will feel better knowing he was murdered, but I don't want to tell her anything until we know what is going on. She has really struggled with his death. His death was the first, then Joe, who was here for a poker competition, then Roberta, who was here for a convention. Tony was a blackjack dealer that worked here, then last month, Ethel, who was a tourist. They had all been ruled accidental until Ethel. For her, we had video that she deliberately stepped out the window. Now, Ella, please ask questions as they occur to you. Trust your instincts."

All eyes in the room swiveled to look at me. I licked my lips, picking up a trace of cold sugar. "Is there anything I should know about how the magic worked on them?"

Olivia tipped her head to the side. "What do you mean?"

"Whatever magic affected them, what kind of rules would it follow? Would they need to be in a place? Touch something? Eat something? Drink something? Perhaps a certain movement? Would the person need a lock of their hair? I don't know enough to know where to start." It felt so weird to casually suggest that someone had performed a spell on these people that resulted in their death. Maybe a floating zeppole to the forehead had gotten me more comfortable with the idea of magic.

Olivia's eyebrows shot up. "Any of those. It really depends on the spell, but it is fair to assume that there was some interaction between the spell caster and the victim. Either direct contact, or the spell caster touched something that the victim touched, or even the victim left something behind that the spell caster used."

I tapped my chin with a finger. "Do you think the interaction occurred at the casino? It would help a lot if we could narrow down our search area."

"Maybe? Spells can be done in a million different ways." She looked around the room, but they only shrugged.

Vanessa scraped her plate sadly then stared longingly at the dessert tray. A gelato started to wobble, when her mom's eyes cut to her, and she shook her head in a firm no.

I was getting excited about the investigation. In many ways, this was similar to the work I used to do and excelled at. The first step was figuring out where to start. "For now, let's assume it happened here at the casino."

Olivia ran a hand down the list. "I know that Ethel was staying here. Joe was competing in a poker tournament here. Roberta was attending a convention in our main ballroom. Vanessa, make a note to see if they were also staying here at the casino. Tony the blackjack dealer was obviously here a lot. We can check if he got a room here or was working that day. Michael used to work here but had been let go a few weeks earlier. He's the only one that I can't say was here for sure. Vanessa, can you make a note."

Falling back on my history of analyzing numbers, I had an idea. "Could we pull credit card receipts for the day of the deaths? Actually, a week or even a month would be better, but I would start by looking at the day of then expand the search if necessary. We can look at patterns of spending to see what they all might have done or places they might have been. Though that doesn't account for any cash they spent. I know that might take a while considering all the stores, departments, entertainment options, and... Can you even get all the receipts? Are some of the places in the casino independently owned?" I pursed my lips.

Olivia's smile grew. "Actually, it will be easy, at least for the people that stayed at the casino. To combat potential theft, when they check in, we snap a picture and give them a card connected to their credit card. They can use it everywhere in the casino, from the slot machines to buying tickets for visiting entertainment in the theaters. They can even tip their servers. We are the safest casino on the Avenue."

"Wow, that's impressive. Did you develop the software just for the casino?"

Olivia smiled. "Yes, but we also invested in a few full-time mages to give some magical insurance to the system."

"Oh!" How quickly I had forgotten the benefits of

being able to use magic. "Can mages automatically recognize other mages?"

"Kinda, sometimes. If someone is actively using magic, then most of us would know. Some people are better at telling than others, and usually, the longer you are around someone and interact, the more likely you will be able to tell, but you might not realize it if you passed one on the street. For instance, when Vin first met you, he didn't know, but when you got mad and insisted that Ramono the Bull was your father, then he started to suspect it was true because he could feel some of your magic."

Vin snorted. "Magic leaking all over the place. She's like a broken sprinkler casting spectral energy all over."

I gave him a dirty look, and he smirked back. He was probably still mad that I had ditched him this morning.

Olivia rolled her eyes at her cousin then turned back to me. "So you want us to pull the charges for each person? What are we looking for?"

"Patterns. Places they all visited. The more details we can get, the better. Did they all use the same slot machine? Visit the same show? Eat the same dessert?" The ideas started to flow, and I started talking faster. I gestured with excitement and accidently knocked over my water glass. "Did they all die in the same way? I know Ethel jumped. What about the rest?"

"In order, Michael overdosed in a parking lot. Joe was diabetic, didn't take his insulin, then fell into a diabetic coma and died. Roberta stepped in front of the Avenue tram and was hit. Tony the blackjack dealer went into the horse stables and was kicked in the head by one of the horses. Lastly was Ethel, who jumped. They all look like accidental deaths, but Dad must have noticed something weird was happening. He pulled those numbers plus the video footage of Ethel the day he was killed."

"Then his death must be connected to these fake suicides?"

A tear dripped off Olivia's nose and landed on her

empty plate to mingle with the powdered sugar. "Running a casino, especially one this big, means you have a target on your back. Plus, it isn't our only financial investment. Not to mention the infighting within the magical community."

My ears perked up. Was I in danger? Was that why Dad hadn't told me I was a witch? I opened my mouth to ask, but Patagonia jumped in my lap and rubbed against my face. She placed a paw on each shoulder and dug her claws into the fabric before rubbing her face all over mine. She kept going until I forcefully pushed her down then used the napkin to wipe off the mascara she had smeared. My makeup had taken quite a beating.

Olivia composed herself. "Even yesterday when you made the connection between the dates and the accidental death payouts, I wasn't convinced the connection was correct and they were all murders. All of the deaths could be accidental, including Ethel, despite what the news said. Maybe she was drunk and fell. But watching the video and hearing your interpretation of events... Well, it just makes too much sense to ignore. We are pulling the financial records. What else?"

"Should I visit the locations and see if I can read them? I mean, like what I did for Ethel?" I wasn't sure what terminology to use.

"Yes, perfect. This morning, I made arrangements to pull the footage from each incident and to mark the location with under construction signs."

"Doesn't that mean that everyone in the casino will know what we are doing within a few hours? I thought you wanted to keep it a secret."

She gave me a sly smile. "I used some persuasion on non-magical people so they will do it but not give it much thought or repeat the story. Since we know a mage is behind this, that should help us, but we will do our best to use back passageways and stay out of sight."

"Do you think whoever is behind this is here?" I

looked toward the door, wondering if someone would bust through at any second.

"Could be. This is another area that is pretty open-ended, depending on how the spell was cast." She tipped her head to the side and stared at the ceiling. "I think it is likely that the caster is at the casino at some point in the days prior to the accident. If it was one person that was targeted and there was a lot of magic involved, then the distance could be farther and the time of interaction longer, but… if I was going to do it, I would be efficient. What do you think?" She looked around the room.

Vanessa shrugged. "Sure. That sounds good."

Auntie Ann smiled. "You're doing great, honey. I think that is a good assumption to start."

Vin nodded. "That's how I would do it."

Olivia stood a bit taller. She had only taken over the casino since her father died, and she appeared to still need the encouragement of her family. "So yes, the mage involved is probably at the casino."

I jotted a note. "So it could be an employee?"

She let out a sigh. "Yes, but it could be anyone that walks in the door."

"Could someone pull the video footage and see if the same person is in the casino in the three days prior to each accident?"

Vin snorted. "Tens of thousands of people come through the casino every day. Even with magic, it would take—Ouch!" He spun to face his mother. "Did you kick me?"

"Of course not, dear. I think that is a good idea, Ella, but it would take too long. But if we narrow down to a suspect, we could do that." She smiled sweetly at me.

Vin scowled and leaned over to rub his leg.

Olivia shook her head. "The fact that it's a mage makes me think it's personal. That the person behind this is targeting my father or the family."

I might not have any magical training, but I did know

people. "Since your father is gone, does that mean there is a chance that they will give up?"

"Maybe, but we can't risk it. Plus, I want whoever did this to pay. Anything else?"

I doodled on the notebook. "That's all I can think of for now."

Auntie Ann brought over a crème brûlée. "You are doing an excellent job. Eat this. You'll need the sugar. Anything else, Olivia? What did Angela say?"

I tapped the sugar crust on the dessert and scooped out the pale dessert with specks of vanilla. The silky-smooth texture and delicate flavor made me moan. I closed my eyes and could smell freshly cut grass and a gentle breeze. It was like being in a garden. I went to take another bite and caught Vin watching with annoyance. I licked the spoon with a longer, more satisfied moan that should have sounded like that scene from *When Harry Met Sally* but, judging from the expression on Vin's face, might have sounded like a patient in the hospital, suffering from cholera.

Vin narrowed his eyes at me then looked at Olivia. "You talked to Angela? What did she say?"

"She said hi to you and said you should call her."

He growled. "You know what I meant."

I looked up in surprise. She must be a lion tamer if she was trying to flirt with Vin. "Who's Angela?"

Vanessa quit spinning in her chair. "She's like you. She can read emotional holograms, but she costs five hundred dollars an hour. And she has the hots for Vinny and is really pretty."

My eyebrows shot up. "If you know someone that does this professionally, shouldn't she be doing this? Is it the cost?"

"It's *not* the cost. She's been doing this for years and is the best around, so don't get any ideas that five hundred an hour is the standard rate." Olivia glared at Vanessa. "She's booked through the next seven months. She was able to squeeze in two hours this morning for me as a favor."

Five hundred dollars an hour was a good reason to work hard at training. "What did she say?"

"We actually covered most of her suggestions of how to start the investigation. The one area you didn't mention was the victims. She said that it is worth our time to see if there is something in their personality or life that tied them together. Magic is more effective when its focus is narrow."

"Isn't that what we're doing by looking to see if they visited the same place in the casino or did the same thing or ate the same food?"

She flipped through her notes. "Those are all things they did. She suggested we investigate to see who they are. This was her example: 'The spell can be more efficient if there is a theme that is personal to the caster. Example: the caster is an only child, and the targets are all only children.' As she explained, these kinds of personal ties make the spell more powerful at the cost of making the caster more obvious. We have an information gatherer pulling together obituaries and any other information we can find out about the people. We should have some answers in the future."

Vanessa leaned forward and caught her mom's eye. "I was thinking that I could hang out with Ella and help her. It would be—"

Her mother cut her off with a wave of the hand. "No, your time is best spent researching."

Vanessa fell back in her chair with a huff that turned to satisfaction when a plate of tiramisu landed in front of her with a thud.

Olivia slammed her notebook shut. "Vanessa is going to request each of the people's records of what they bought here at the casino. Vin is going to check in to see how the locations are being secured. Auntie Ann is going to see how the information gathering is going, and lastly, you and I are going to check on one quick thing before we meet Vin to see if there is any emotional hologram left at any of the locations."

CHAPTER EIGHT

Olivia unlocked a door at the end of the hallway from her office. Vin, Auntie Ann, and Vanessa had ducked into separate offices all down the hall. Patagonia squeezed through the door ahead of us. I followed Olivia in, and the cold of the room hit my face like an arctic blast.

I wrapped my arms around my middle. "Wow, it's really cold in here." My breath frosted briefly in front of me.

Olivia flipped on the lights. "What? Oh, I guess. Dad liked it cold. This is his office. Was his office."

The office was similar to Olivia's but larger and more impressive. Tasteful artwork hung on the wall. An enormous desk dominated the room. There was stillness there that was palpable. "You haven't moved anything in here, have you?" I stepped behind the desk and gasped. The carpet was black with blood.

"No. Can you get anything from the room? Can you tell me what happened to my father? We don't have a camera in here, so anything you can tell me will help." Olivia's voice carried a note of desperation and the edges of a little girl. She quickly dabbed at her shiny eyes with her sleeve.

"Okay, I'll try." I slipped the channeling key into my hand, and Patagonia rubbed up against my leg before I could even call her over. I took a long, deep breath, closed my eyes, and cleared my mind.

I was starting to think that last time was a fluke, when emotions and images started slowly leaking into my consciousness. The physical world started to recede. I could barely feel Patagonia sitting on my feet. There was a faint sound of a door creaking open. A conversation started around me, but it was nothing beyond a rumble that faded to static as I started to focus on the room.

It was icy cold. And a wave of anger and hatred spread over me. It felt like black tar but bitter and rancid in my mouth. It receded slightly as an image came to me of a man hunched over his desk, examining pages. I recognized the papers as the ones Olivia had shown me. The vision was a mix of senses. I smelled the bitter black coffee on his desk but could also taste it in my mouth. I heard the papers rustling but could also feel them under my fingers.

I was seeing the scene but also experiencing it from his point of view. It was disorienting. He flipped through the pages again then sighed and pulled out a stone egg. He placed the channel key into an indent in the underside of the desk, and an ornate piece of carved wood trim popped away from the desk.

He removed it and pulled from the desk a leather-bound file. On the front, it had an intricate feather and was held shut by a piece of thin string. He opened the file, and at the top was my father's name. I strained to see what was on the paper, but I couldn't get the image to focus beyond his name. The rest of the page was a hazy blur of words.

Suddenly, everything was out of focus, and a terrible cold dread filled the room. The man jerked his head up, but the movement was jerky and slow, as if he was drugged. His vision went hazy and started to darken. He pulled up his power and started to say, "What are you— "

when a large boom ended the vision.

I gasped and opened my eyes to see four people leaning over me. I was prone on the floor and couldn't remember how I got there. "I'm fine. I'm fine."

Vanessa peered over me, her face upside down as she stood behind my head. "You keeled right over. Vinny had to catch you."

I looked at his imposing figure hovering over me. I realized that I was clenching his hand in mine, my knuckles white and my fingernails digging into him. I let my hand go limp, and it fell to the floor as he released it and stood.

"I'll get her some water." He stomped out of the room, the ground vibrating under his footsteps.

Auntie Ann felt my forehead. "How are you feeling?"

"Tired." I jiggled my arms and legs. "Kinda sore, actually."

"What's two plus two?"

"Four? Is that a trick question?" My calves burned as I pointed and flexed each foot.

"Where are you?"

"Olivia's dad's office at the Golden Pyramid Casino in Rambler, Nevada."

"Good." She stood up and dragged Olivia with her to the far corner of the office.

Vanessa opened her mouth to speak, but I held a finger to my lips, and she stopped.

Auntie Ann's voice was meant to be a whisper, but it cut across the room. "What did you think you were doing? I thought we agreed to wait until she had more training. What if there had been some kind of trap set?"

Olivia's voice sounded more like a whiney teenager's than a grown woman's. "I checked, and I figured it wouldn't hurt to try."

"I've trained plenty of mages in my day, and if any one of them—" Her voice dropped, and her words became indecipherable, though her angry tone was clear.

I sighed and slowly sat up. The energy I had at lunch

was replaced with a heavy depression that seemed to materialize from the fog of the vision.

Patagonia meowed and pressed her nose against my shoulder before stomping on it to drag her big, wet tongue over my nape. She started at the baby-fine hairs at the back of my neck. Her tongue was like fine sandpaper, and the odd sensation sent a chill down my spine.

Vanessa patted my back. "Mom's pretty pissed at Olivia. When we came in, you were standing there with this goofy look on your face, then you tipped over. Good thing Vin caught you, or you would have smashed your face. I thought you'd never come around."

"What?" I rubbed my face. "How long was I out?"

"Maybe five minutes. Mom was worried. You know she's a famous teacher? When Uncle Edward died, she came back to Rambler. She had been teaching in Europe. I was with her, studying. She's trying to keep both Olivia and Vinny in line." She rolled her eyes.

"What about you? Is she keeping you in line too?" I teased her.

"I'm an angel." She smirked.

We chuckled, then she offered me her hand to get up. After I stood, I pointed each foot and stretched. "Your whole family works here?"

"Now we do. Vinny used to work at a bunch of places around town, but he's here for now. And Mom is helping Olivia get settled."

"And you?"

"I'm still discovering myself." She gave me a wink, though a little bit of sadness in her eyes shone through.

"Fair enough. You're still young." Patagonia rubbed up against my leg then stretched onto her back legs to claw gently at my stomach. I scratched behind her ears, her purring vibrating my hand. "Your dad?"

"He passed away when I was a kid."

"Wow." Olivia, Vanessa, and I all had dead fathers.

"It's a tough life."

Vin walked in, and there must have been something on both of our faces because he stopped and looked at us. "What?" He bit off the word as an accusation and extended a plastic bottle of water to me.

Auntie Ann came over. "Everyone out. Vanessa, why don't you spend the day with the research team and Vin can catch up on his work. I'm going to go with Olivia and Ella to see what Ella can find."

Vin left before she was done talking.

Vanessa blew out a breath and sulked out the door.

Olivia rushed over. "No, Auntie, that's not necessary."

"It most certainly is. If nothing else, I can start Ella's training." She adjusted her sweater. She was carrying a small purse and pulled out a candy bar that she handed me. She motioned for us to follow. "Eat this while we take the elevator to...?" She turned to Olivia and raised her brow as she pressed the elevator button.

"Oh." Olivia flipped open her tablet. "I figured we would go in reverse order of occurrence since the emotional hologram will fade over time." She stepped into the elevator, ran a security card through the reader, and pressed the button for the basement. "Tony was killed in the stables."

The elevator doors started to close, and I pressed my foot in the way until Patagonia was safely inside. I already found myself constantly scanning any room I was in to locate her, though I found that more often than not, I already had a vague sense of where she was before I looked. "There's a stable here?"

Olivia pressed the door close button, and we started to descend. "Yes, we have horses that are here full time for carriage rides, along with a place for events like barrel racing, horse shows, and the annual alpaca national agility event."

I chuckled. "Alpaca agility?"

Olivia nodded with a smile. "They run little obstacle courses and even have a costume show. Have you ever seen an alpaca dressed up as a dragon? It's something special."

I bit into the chocolate candy bar, the layers of nougat and nuts giving me resistance as I chewed. The sugar hit me hard and washed away the remnants I had felt after my vision. I rolled the memories around in my head. "Olivia, after your father was shot, did they find a leather portfolio with a file about my father on the desk? It had a feather on the front."

She immediately perked up. "No, the only things on the desk were the papers I showed you. What else did you see?" The elevator door started to open.

"No, not now." Auntie Ann stepped out of the elevator.

"Please, Auntie, I just want to know if I was right that it was murder." Olivia turned to me.

I nodded.

A single tear trickled down her face, and she blew out a sigh. "I feel better just to know for sure. And what—"

The elevator started to close, but Auntie Ann stepped to block the door. "Later, Olivia. I know you are upset. I miss my brother also, but someone's life is hanging in the balance until we find out who is doing this and stop them. But I promise we will come back to this."

"You're right." Olivia stepped out of the elevator and across the hall to swipe a card and pull open a door.

I followed her and went through the open door. The scent of hay and animals filled my lungs, and I breathed deeply. Patagonia meowed and raced ahead to the end of an aisle, where she batted at loose hay. She knocked it into the air then leapt after it, twisting to pounce on top of it. Her white fangs glinted as she wrestled and chomped on the yellow straw.

I chuckled and thought of Monterey, California. My family had taken me in my teens, and my favorite had been the otters that played in the water. Patagonia's playful side reminded me of them. She pranced back to me and presented the piece of straw on my shoe. I reached down and picked it up, scratching her behind the ears as a thank-you before returning to the task at hand.

"Maybe I should write down what I saw. What if I forget?" The burden of her father's death weighed heavily on me, not to mention the file about my father. How did it fit in? Where did it go?

Auntie Ann bent over and grabbed a long stalk of straw to tease Patagonia, who had gone to her side and danced to reach to bobbing plant. "Visions are like memories. It is there inside you. In the environment, the emotional hologram may degrade over time, but your vision of it will stay intact. You're not ready to read it, but I'll train you, and you will be soon."

We turned down an aisle. Horses hung their heads over the stalls, gently nickering as we went by. As a child, I had worshipped horses. I wanted to stop and stroke their soft noses, but Olivia and Auntie Ann did not slow down. Toward the end of the aisle, there were several empty stalls then caution tape marking off the last three stalls before the dead end.

Olivia held down the tape and stepped over it. We followed, and as we approached the last stall on the left, I slowed down. Inside, something huffed and snorted. The ground shook as hooves stomped, and then something hit the door, rattling it on the hinges.

I edged away from the stall but kept progressing forward until I could see over the stall door into the interior. An enormous black horse circled inside before turning its back to us and kicking back at the door again. One of the bolts on the door's hinges pulled away from the frame.

Acrid sweat filled the air and shone on the black fur of the animal. His mane was long but tangled and knotted in large chunks.

"No! Get away!" A man ran down the aisle toward us. "Ladies, please, you must—Oh, Miss Santini, I'm so sorry, but I must implore you to come away from Hercules. He's not well. Please."

Hercules whinnied and stomped before slamming into the door, the top edge cutting into his chest. He bared his teeth and snapped at the air.

The gentleman was older, with sinewy strength in his arms exposed by a short-sleeve shirt. He looked at Hercules with sadness. "We don't know what's wrong with him. We're going to have to put him down. He's starting to hurt himself."

"What?" Olivia turned to him in surprise. "What's going on? Why hadn't I heard anything?"

"I'm sorry. With your father passing, no one wanted to bother you. We've tried everything."

Olivia stared into the stall as Hercules continued to snort and pace. "When did this start?"

He rubbed his temples. "Since that young man was killed. We could barely get his body out of the stall. That's when I got this." He lifted a sleeve to reveal a scar that extended from his shoulder to his elbow. It was still scabbed over in spots, and the healed places were red and angry in their healing.

"I'm so sorry, Vladimir. We will stay back, but can we have some time alone?"

He hesitated before answering. "Please just be careful. The vet is coming soon to put him out of his suffering." He turned and slowly shuffled down the aisle and disappeared.

Auntie Ann tapped her chin. "Something isn't right. Hercules has always been such a gentle horse. Vanessa used to ride him bareback around the arena. He took such good care of her. And he just happened to start acting up since Tony was killed?"

She closed her eyes and breathed deeply, the way she had shown me. I did the same. I started picking up emotions and sensations immediately but very differently than I had before. Instead of echoes of emotions, the feelings were very present and centered on the enormous horse stomping around in his stall in front of me. Fear, anger, and disgust all fought inside the body of the black beast.

I ran my tongue over my mouth, trying to clear it of the foul taste, as though I had sucked on a battery. "What is that?"

Auntie Ann's eyes flew open. "You can sense that?"

"Yes, but it's different from Mr. Santini's office or where Ethel jumped. Why?"

Auntie Ann started digging around in her large purse. "Because this is not something from the past. This is happening right now. Someone has cursed this horse."

"The same person that is killing everyone?" I guessed.

"That seems likely. We will need to remove it from the poor animal. Where is it?" She started taking fistfuls of things from her purse and shoving them at Olivia. "All those awful feelings need to go somewhere. It would work best if we put them onto something living, but that is too cruel. But you can find something that was alive and has the potential for life like a fruit. It was living, and the seeds have the potential for more life. Here it is!" She pulled from her purse a large orange that she placed on the ground then stood and grabbed my hands.

"What are we doing?"

The horse kicked at the stall, but his eyes showed pain and suffering hidden behind all the stomping and snorting.

"You are going to help me. I'm not sure if you have a second affinity for animals or emotions or what, but we don't have time to figure it out. The burden on that horse is too great. It's been two months, and his heart might not take much more. We'll close our eyes and try to push the curse from the horse to the orange. Come, Patagonia, Ella will need you."

Patagonia sat on my feet. "Uh, I think I'm going to need more instruction."

"I'm doing the heavy lifting. You're just going to give

me a little oomph. Grab your channeling key."

I dropped her hand to grab the smooth moonstone in my palm before holding her hand again, the stone between us. I took a slow, deep breath and closed my eyes. "Now what?"

"Picture the horse and the orange. Now imagine pushing the negative things off the horse and onto the orange. Don't grab it. Just push with your mind."

I mumbled, "Oh, obviously."

She squeezed my hand. "If all you do is stand here with me, you will be a help. We begin."

Hercules snorted and kicked. The smell of his sweat filled my lungs. While forming a mental picture of him and the orange, I wrestled with what Auntie Ann had asked me to do. I reached out and felt until I could clearly sense the hatred and fear on the horse, then I shoved at it with my mind, pushing it toward the orange. Forever, it felt as if nothing was happening. I imagined heaving, pulling, twisting, and every other variation of moving the sensation, but I didn't feel any difference.

Hercules was becoming more agitated in his stall, but he wasn't the only one. Auntie Ann's breathing was getting labored, and her fingers delicately trembled.

I redoubled my effort, but my mind was starting to wander, and as I was losing the focus, my method changed. Instead of pushing directly at the horse, my effort slipped along the outside of it, and something shifted. Auntie Ann's hand twitched in mine. She felt it too. I focused my effort on pushing on the outside of the horse, like wiping my hand over his coat to push off water.

I continued around my mental picture of the horse, wiping it off. Auntie Ann must have been moving it from there because once it disconnected from the horse, it was whisked to the orange before I could push any farther. I went over the whole body then down the legs and up the neck to the face. My energy was wearing out, and the channeling key was hot in my hand, but I continued.

Auntie Ann let out a deep sigh. "You can stop. It's done."

I opened my eyes and blinked. It could have been a minute or an hour that we had stood there. I didn't know which. My knees ached, and I ran a hand over my lower back.

Olivia walked Auntie Ann over to a chair. "Was it bad?"

She nodded and dug out two candy bars. After biting and chewing one, she swallowed hard. "Yes, whoever cast that curse is very powerful. I wasn't expecting that. Here, dear, eat this." She extended the second candy bar to me.

I opened the wrapper and bit through the chocolate shell and into the caramel and nut center. The sugar hit my blood and made my skin tingle. Patagonia meowed, and I scooped up her massive wiggly frame to press my cheek against her neck. She purred into my ear and flexed her paws rhythmically against my shoulders. I struggled under her weight and was about to put her down when she yowled and clawed her way out of my arms and climbed onto my shoulder, draping herself around my neck like a furry stole.

Olivia looked at me then back at her aunt. "Did Ella help?"

"Yes, very much. If I had known it would be that difficult, I would have had you help, Olivia." She finished off the candy and pulled out a compact to reapply her lipstick. The color had returned to her face, and she seemed right as rain. "I think Ella has a natural affinity for the work. She was able to loosen the edges of the curse. I did all the heavy lifting, so to speak, but I'm impressed with her knack for the delicate work."

Patagonia was done being my neckwear and meowed loudly in my ear. I lifted her off me and lowered her to the ground, letting her jump from the height of my hip. She hit the floor and smoothly moved toward the stall.

I followed her over. Hercules was slick with sweat

reflecting the lights in the stable. His head hung low, his lower lip dangling down and his tongue poking out. His eyes were half closed until he caught sight of me.

He nickered softly and slowly stepped over, his massive hooves dragging lightly through the straw in his stall. He shook his massive head, his mane slapping on each side of his neck, and tendrils sticking to the sweat. I extended my hand palm up, and he lifted his head over the stall door to nestle into my palm. His lips were velvety soft.

I reached up to scratch behind his massive ears. He closed his eyes and blew air and snot out of his nose.

The stomping of boots racing across the floor echoed in the aisle. "Hercules!" Vladimir ran up but slowed as he approached. "Is he…?"

Hercules nickered, and I stepped back. "I think he is feeling better."

Vladimir extended his hand and ran it over the horse's face. "Old friend, you're back." He grabbed a halter off a hook hanging next to the door and pulled it over Hercules's nose then wrapped the strap over behind the ears then through a buckle.

I tried to think of an excuse for the horse's sudden change in behavior. "Oh, he… The thing is that I—"

"No. I have worked here long enough to know that I don't need to know. Thank you." He opened the door and pulled the horse out by the lead. "Thank you, Miss Olivia. Thank you, Mrs. Russo."

CHAPTER NINE

I leaned against the elevator and hid a yawn behind my hand. In the hours since helping Hercules, we had investigated two more of the deaths. First we had taken the elevator up to where Roberta had been the third victim. She had been attending a convention, and a group of friends had gone to the tram station to visit the other casinos. An express tram was about to race through the station when Roberta had surged forward in front of the tram and been killed instantly.

Her companions insisted that it must have been an accident as she had been in a great mood and laughing just a moment earlier, but the video showed that she definitely hadn't tripped but instead stepped off the platform.

When I had closed my eyes, I felt something similar to what Ethel had felt. There was love and happiness. Roberta hadn't suffered, and whatever she stepped toward had brought her great joy.

After we had watched the video and I had read the area as many times as I could, we took the elevator up to where the second death had occurred. Joe had been playing in the poker tournament that weekend. He had come upstairs to the floor his room was on, but instead of going there, he had stepped into an alcove with a chair, sat down, and never moved again. He was severely diabetic, and when he didn't check his blood sugar and take his insulin, he had slipped into a coma and passed before anyone checked on him.

The video didn't show anything useful. When I went to read the emotional hologram, it was very weak and faded. I had struggled for a long time trying to get any details, but in the end I just picked up a general sense of warmth and happiness, like sipping on a cup of hot chocolate or slipping into a warm bath.

Last, we were going down to see if there was anything I could discover at the site of the first death. Patagonia was taking an aptly named cat nap at my feet in the elevator, and I finished the last bit of taffy. I had never ingested so much sugar in one day. My stomach was turning sour, and it was no longer providing the energy lift of earlier.

I ran my finger over a small scratch in the hand rail of the elevator. Up and down all day, I was quite familiar with every detail of the elevator. In a casino this size, they must have dozens of elevators, and yet we only had to use one elevator to visit all five locations.

"Could the elevator be involved?" I asked as the door dinged open.

"Pardon?" Auntie Ann reached into her purse and pulled out a package of gummy bears and offered them to me as we walked through the casino.

I shook my head. "If I eat any more sugar, I'll throw up."

She put them back and offered me a bottle of water instead. "You'll sleep well tonight."

Olivia slowed down so we could catch up. "What did you mean about the elevator?"

"We have used the same elevator to investigate all the deaths. Ethel took it to the abandoned floor where she jumped, it was next to the horse that trampled Tony, it's the nearest to the tram station, Joe used it to get to his room, and now we took it to the parking lot to see where Michael overdosed. Maybe the elevator is cursed or the source."

Olivia slowed, and her eyebrows knitted together. "Maybe… but the elevator isn't the closest to the parking garage, so it must be a coincidence."

"But maybe Michael took it anyways. This could be the thing that ties all five cases together."

"Four." Olivia pushed on past the slot machines and disappeared into the crowd around a roulette table.

I coughed and ran a hand across my forehead. I was feeling feverish.

Auntie Ann took the empty water bottle from my hand and replaced it with a fresh one. Her massive purse seemed to hold everything in it. "You've done a lot of magic today for someone who has never done any before. What were you saying to Olivia?"

I unscrewed the top, drank half of it, and let out a loud burp. "I was just spit-balling an idea, but Olivia didn't listen." I finished the water while thinking about her reaction. "She seemed distracted."

Auntie Ann turned to find Olivia and found something significant. "Oh boy. I think you're right. Come along." She walked off in the direction Olivia had gone.

I tossed the empty plastic container into the trash and emptied out my pockets of candy wrappers before scooping Patagonia into my arms. It appeared that people in general were giving her a wide berth, but I worried about the increasing drunken crowds near the card tables.

Staggering under her weight, I weaved through the crowd. She seemed heavier than before, or perhaps I was getting weaker. She didn't help me any as she obscured my view by rubbing her face against mine. I sneezed when her black hair tickled my nose. Once I was through the rows of blackjack, craps, and roulette tables, the crowd thinned to a few people spread over probably a hundred slot machines. The machines rang and flashed, trying to seduce me into lightening my wallet.

I loosened my grip on Patagonia, and she leapt down to race down the strip of carpeting that designated the walkway. Trotting after her, I spied Olivia and Auntie near the entry to the parking garage, talking to Vin and another man. The second gentleman was the same height as Vin but tall and slim, as opposed to Vin's broad shoulders and muscular chest, but both of them radiated power.

They turned and left before I could reach them, which was for the better since Vin's bad attitude had been annoying. He thought he was so cool, important, and hot. "Who was that with Vin?"

Olivia looked at me, startled out of whatever deep thoughts she had been having. "No one important. Come on. This is the last place, then we're done for today." She pressed open the door to the garage and marched on.

Auntie Ann caught the door and held it open for me. "Don't mind Olivia. She's got a lot on her mind. Make sure you get a lot of protein tonight. Sugar is good for keeping up your energy, but you need real food."

"So eating two pounds of candy isn't healthy? I never would have guessed," I teased her.

Auntie Ann chuckled and gave me a smile.

We walked along the long rows of cars. I should have brought Patagonia's harness and leash. Though she followed by my side, I could just imagine a car swinging around a corner and not seeing her. She was enormous for a cat but still so much smaller than a person.

I slapped my thigh, and she bounded over before twining herself between my legs as I tried to walk. I stumbled and tried to catch myself before I face-planted. I flung out a hand that landed on the trunk of an expensive red sports car. Immediately, the parking garage echoed with honking from the car's alarm bouncing around the cement structure.

A young man in a uniform came running around the corner. "Ma'am, this is the valet area. Can I assist you in—

73

Hello, Ms. Russo, Miss Santini. I apologize. I didn't see that she was with you."

Olivia turned back and approached. "I'm so sorry about the car alarm. It won't happen again." She turned to glare at me.

I shrugged. It was hardly as if I did it on purpose.

"Miss Santini, I put up the tape like you asked." He pointed to the end of the row, where several caution cones barred traffic from going around the corner. "But the next show starts in two hours, and the valet area is starting to fill up. We hate to turn away customers, but…" He looked around at the cars around us.

"I'm taking care of it right now. We need another thirty minutes or so."

He nodded. "Why don't I take the cones down now, but I won't let the boys park any of the cars on this level until the other spots are all filled. Thank you."

As we passed the safety cones and turned the corner, he stopped and collected the cones, then his retreating jogging steps indicated he had left.

I walked past the empty parking spots and took out the channeling key and started taking slow, deep breaths. Even with only one day of practice, the peace and ease I needed to work magic was coming faster.

"Here." Olivia pulled out her tablet and cued up the video as she had at every location.

I touched Play, and the recording of the empty parking structure started. A disheveled, lanky man stumbled to his car, parked in the spot where we were standing. He got into his car, and the tablet cut off.

I pressed the button, and it flashed a picture of a battery. "It's dead."

Olivia snatched it back with more force than necessary. "Seriously?" She jabbed at the button.

"Is there anyone specific that I needed to see?"

"Not really. He gets in the car, and that's all we can see. One of the valets found him later. Michael had overdosed.

The video doesn't show anything. Don't know why I even bothered to show you." She shoved the tablet in her purse. Her hand got caught on one of the straps, and she fought with the purse, growling, until finally she seated the purse back on her shoulder.

Auntie Ann cut her eyes over to Olivia but didn't comment on her growing agitation.

Patagonia rubbed against my leg, and the channeling key's smooth finish was growing warm in my hand. "Why don't I see what I can find?"

"Yes. Fine."

I closed my eyes and expected to find something, but there was nothing to feel. The space was empty and clean. My nostrils tickled from fumes but nothing magical. I spent several minutes trying before a shrill voice broke my concentration.

"What are you doing here?"

I opened my eyes to see Isadora. She had caught us in the spot where her son had died.

Olivia blanched. "We were walking Ella to her car when she got light-headed."

Isadora narrowed her eyes. "I've seen you all over the casino."

I could feel Isadora's suspicion growing. They had wanted to keep my investigation quiet, but maybe a good red herring would help. "It was a secret, but I'm doing a financial audit."

Her suspicion changed. It was less hostile. My excuse was working.

"We weren't going to tell anyone, but since you already caught us, I might as well explain. Miss Santini asked me to come in and look over ways that the casino could cut costs. I'll be here for a week. I've been getting over the flu, though, and I had to take a little break on the way to my car." I faked a weak cough.

"Oh, that makes sense." She visibly relaxed.

Olivia grabbed onto the lie. "Yes. I didn't want to say

anything before, so please don't tell anyone."

Isadora nodded.

"In fact, don't be surprised if you see her undercover this week, investigating a few places." She put a hand on my arm and pulled me away. "Goodbye, Isadora."

We said goodbyes, and I allowed Olivia to drag me out of sight of Isadora before I reclaimed my arm. "Undercover?"

"Just covering all my bases. What did you sense before she interrupted?"

"Nothing." I rubbed my temples.

"What do you mean?"

"I'm sorry. I didn't feel a thing. Nothing. Not even a whisper. I'm sorry. I really tried."

"Here." Auntie Ann offered me another candy bar. "If you didn't feel anything, then the hologram is probably too faded. They don't last forever."

I raised my hand, refusing the take the candy bar. "No, thank you. I already feel sick. What if I just missed something?" I was feeling unsure... and nauseated.

Her heels clicked along next to me as we navigated the parking garage. "If you say you didn't feel anything, then trust that. Where's your car?"

"One floor up."

"Olivia, I'll meet you back at the office. I want to see Ella to her car."

"Sure thing, Auntie." Olivia pulled open a door, and sounds of slot machines filled the parking garage. "Tomorrow. Nine a.m. My office." She jabbed a finger in my direction then left, the door slamming behind her.

Auntie Ann walked to the stairs and beckoned me on. "Why did you decide to tell Isadora that you were doing a financial audit?"

I trotted up the stairs behind her then turned right toward my car while triple-checking that Patagonia was still safely by my side. "She seemed suspicious, and I *was* hired to do a financial audit, so I figured a near truth would be safest. This is my car."

"You have good instincts and magic. Trust that. Now go home and rest." She smiled.

I thanked her and got in the car to do as she said.

CHAPTER TEN

This time I recognized the little bells that filled the loft. I was lying on my side on top of my bed, still in my clothes from the day. Patagonia was purring loudly, her head wedged under my chin and her body pressed up against my chest like a furry body pillow. I stretched my arms over me as my stomach growled loudly. I pressed a hand to my midsection, and it was hollowed in, unlike the normal soft flesh I had from too many doughnuts. Working magic might be the best diet I had ever tried.

I grabbed my phone and checked the messages. I had a long list of missed calls and a text from Vin.

Opening my phone, I pulled up the text. "I'm at the door."

I was debating rolling over and going back to sleep when a second message came in and the doorbell rang again.

This text was more intriguing. "Mom sent over food for you."

My stomach growled, and I slowly crawled off the bed.

Patagonia leapt to the floor and raced to the front door while I grabbed a stick of gum off the bookshelf and followed behind.

It was dark outside, and my phone said it was ten p.m. I felt slightly refreshed from my nap but was eager to crawl back into my bed once I had eaten.

I checked the peephole at the door. Vin pressed the doorbell again and started texting on his phone.

I pulled the door open, and the smell of garlic bread hit me like a ton of bricks.

"Here." He handed me a paper bag then pushed past me with another bag in his hand and a huge duffel bag thrown over one shoulder.

As I closed the door behind him, Patagonia stood on her back legs, yowling and clawing to tear the bag open.

I lifted it up out of her reach and padded after him. Peeking into the huge brown paper bag, I grabbed a breadstick, the outside greasy with warm butter and herbs. After biting into it, I paused to moan and close my eyes. The crisp outside broke under my teeth while the center was soft. Garlic tickled my mouth with its delicate flavoring. I stood there to finish it in peace before rooting around in the bag to uncover several containers of pasta in Alfredo or red sauce and a salad dressed in Italian dressing, the tang of vinegar tickling my nose.

"This looks amazing." I was tempted to open up a container and eat it right there with my hand but was able to control the urge. I entered the kitchen and pulled out plates. "Are you eating too?"

"That's the plan. Get started if you want while I cook the meat." He also had a pan on the stove and was going through my cupboards.

I pulled out some plates and silverware then dished some of the pasta onto my plate. I fell upon the food, barely holding back from stuffing it into my mouth. The flavors danced in my mouth, and I moaned again with pleasure. "This is so good. Is it from Isadora's?"

Patagonia jumped onto the counter and dove for the food but I grabbed her around the middle and swung her off. She meowed and wailed until I took a tiny bit of food and placed it in the bowl on the floor for her. She gave me a look and tapped the side of the bowl with her paw. I ladled in more food. If this was how she ate, it was no surprise that I could barely carry her around. She would be a blimp within a week.

"No, Mom made it just for us. She wanted to steer clear of Isadora's for a bit, plus she says these recipes have always been good for restoring your strength."

I twirled fettuccine onto my fork. "I appreciate the food. It's amazing, but why... uh... why are you here?"

"I'm spending the night." He pulled out a white package from the bag. After unfolding the white butcher paper, he pulled out two circular cuts of red meat and placed them in the hot pan. They sizzled, and he added salt and pepper to the meat.

"No, you're not spending the night." The smell of the meat in the pan made my mouth water even as I was eating. "What is that?"

"Filet mignon, and yes I am." He said it with no more emotions than if he were telling me the time. It was a statement of fact.

"I think I get to decide who spends the night." Anger was creeping into my voice. Not only was I annoyed that he thought he was spending the night, but also the fact that he believed he got to decide the matter.

He used a pair of tongs to flip the meat, the second side hissing as it met the hot pan. He pulled out plates and silverware. "Do you know my job?"

My curiosity was increasing, but so was my irritation. "Not really, but that doesn't matter—"

"I do security at the casino, not just the Golden Pyramid, but several of our family's casinos, and I consult elsewhere. Do you know why I'm so good?"

I blew out a sigh and dropped my protests for now. "No. Why are you 'so good'?" I made air quotes with my fingers to accentuate that they were his words, not mine.

He smirked a little and moved the steaks onto plates

then handed me one. "I know when trouble is coming. When to double up on security for an event. When to pay special attention to a department. When a particular client or employee is about to cause trouble. And right now, trouble is coming. Don't cut into that now. It needs to rest."

The kitchen was separated from the rest of the loft by a chest-height bar with stools underneath. I had sat down to dig into the steak, but at his warning, I rolled my eyes and put my knife and fork down. "Of course trouble is coming. Another murder is about to happen."

He opened my refrigerator and shifted things around until he pulled out two beers. Using his keys, he took off the tops then placed one in front of me. "No, the trouble is centered around you. It's probably related to the investigation of the murder, but the trouble is heading toward you." He took a long pull off the beer. "It's a good sign. Means we are probably headed in the right direction, but inconvenient because I need to babysit you."

"No one needs to babysit me."

He turned the full weight of his glare on me. He held my eyes while I struggled to not look away. I felt like a tiny dog staring down a massive pit bull. The hairs on the back of my neck lifted, but I pressed my lips into a thin line. No matter how intimidating he was, I wasn't going to be bullied in my own home by anyone. As the seconds ticked by, my irritation grew. He was clearly used to being in charge of every situation, but no one was in charge of me. I imagined someone trying this on my father, and my resolve grew.

I was ready to chew him out when a large black creature leapt onto the counter. At first glance, I thought it was Patagonia, and I opened my mouth to yell, but when I turned to face her, I gasped instead. This cat was twice the size. It raced across the countertop, snatching the meat off Vin's plate, then used its powerful hind legs to launch itself to the top of the cabinets then to one of the beams that ran across the loft.

Patagonia looked up from her bowl of food and let out a screech. She took off running, and within a few moments, she was racing across the beam to face the intruder. She yowled and growled. They faced each other, and I could see the differences. The other cat was twice as big but also heavier set, with a wide chest, bulkier head, and strong muscular shoulders and hips. While Patagonia was delicate and slender, this cat was pure muscle.

"Aristotle!" Vin growled.

"You know... that?" I pointed at the creature.

The scruff of its neck lifted as Patagonia swiped at its nose.

I screamed and crawled up onto the countertop. I danced over the plates of food to shake my fists and wave at the creature. If it attacked Patagonia, it could easily kill her with one shake. "No! Leave her alone."

"He won't kill her. He can't, at least not like this. They're just figuring each other out." He raised his voice. "Aristotle! Give that back."

"What is he?" My stomach was still in my throat as Patagonia swiped across his nose again, drawing a bright-red line of blood. He pulled back, ears pressed flat against his head.

"My familiar."

"You brought him without telling me?" The growling and hissing had died down, and the large cat tore the steak in half and laid the pieces down on the beam. Patagonia grabbed one piece, her white teeth gleaming in contrast to the pink meat, then she raced out of sight deeper into the loft, with Aristotle padding silently behind her.

"No, I didn't. I've told you that already. You don't have to bring them anywhere. They go exactly where they please. I guess he decided to join me same way that Patagonia came to the casino."

"You mean by magic? Just poof, and there she is?"

He reached up and grabbed me around the hips and

lifted me off the counter. I lurched and grabbed his shoulders so he wouldn't drop me, but he was stronger than I thought. He pulled me close and lowered me, my body barely grazing his. If I arched my back, I would be pressed up against him, our curves meeting in all the right places. My feet hit the ground. I swallowed hard and stepped away, a bit shaky in the legs.

"After using magic all day, you're surprised?" He grabbed my steak and cut it in half before placing one piece in front of me and keeping the other half for himself. "I can't believe he stole my meal."

"He's enormous." I cut into the meat and bit into a piece. The meat gave under my teeth, and I couldn't hold back a moan of pleasure. "This is amazing. Thank you."

He nodded and started into his own food. "You can tell his size?"

I swallowed my food and was torn between taking another bite and answering. My curiosity won out. "He's enormous. How couldn't I notice his size? I thought some jungle cat had broken in." I barely got out the last word before I stuffed another bite into my mouth.

"To non-magical humans, he looks the same size as Patagonia. But witches see his magical ability." He pulled over the bag of food he had given me and scooped a large helping onto his plate where the steak had been.

"So is he a large cat that looks small to non-witches, or is he the size of Patagonia and looks bigger to witches?"

He shrugged. "That's a question for the philosophers. I just know that he steals all the covers."

I stifled a yawn. With my belly full again, my eyelids were heavy. "About you spending the night. I don't—"

"Trust me. I don't want to be here either. I had to cancel a date, but I told Mom that I would keep an eye on you. She feels uneasy as well." He grabbed my empty plate and his own and went to the sink.

I opened my mouth to argue, but a yawn interrupted me.

"Look. They figured things out." Vin pointed past me.

Patagonia and Aristotle were on the couch. The enormous cat lay on the couch with his eyes closed, and Patagonia was licking one of his ears before wedging herself between him and the back cushion. Their combined purring filled the air.

"Fine. You can crash on the couch. But just…" The idea of him sleeping here unsettled me, but I couldn't figure out how to express that. "Stay out of trouble."

"Wait." He scraped a lonely fettuccine noodle into the trash and wrapped up the remains of the garlic bread. "There is something else we need to discuss about tomorrow."

I stopped short. "What?"

Before he could reply, the doorbell rang. I looked at him and arched an eyebrow, but he shrugged. I went to the door and used the peephole. Lou Freeman from the security firm on the floor below my loft was at the door. I recognized his formidable beard and burly build.

I opened the door. "Hi, Lou. Can I help you?"

"So sorry to disturb you, but someone heard you scream. Are you okay?" He searched my face intently.

"Yes, yes, I'm fine. I was just startled."

He started to say something then cut himself off when he looked over my shoulder. "Vin."

Vin's strong presence behind me was like a fire at my back. The heat of his body pressed up against me, though when I turned around, he was still several feet away. His energy took up more space than his body.

He nodded. "Lou."

I looked between them. "You guys know each other?"

Neither of them spoke for a long time until Vin finally replied, "Security's a small field. I'll let you two talk."

After Vin had returned to the kitchen and he wasn't directly in sight of the door, I turned back to Lou. "Thank you for checking on me, but I'm fine." My cheeks grew hot as I realized that it looked as though Vin was spending the night for other reasons than security, but I couldn't possibly explain why he was really here. Lamely, I added, "He's sleeping on the couch."

He caught my eyes and held them. "Can you come to my office alone tomorrow to talk? I have some security concerns."

I shook my head. I needed to finish the investigation first then figure out things with my dad and this whole magical witch situation. "Not tomorrow, but soon. Thank you for stopping by and checking on me." I started to pull the door shut.

He wedged a foot into the door and waited. He wasn't moving until I committed to a firm time. And neither was I, since I couldn't leave the door open all night.

My father had lived above Lou's office for years. Maybe Lou knew something that would be useful to me. We had never talked about my father, instead focusing on making sure my loft was safe or the building was running correctly. "I'm busy the next two days, but I can come over the first thing after that."

He nodded and left without another word or sound.

I closed and locked the door behind him. I was going to need to figure out how to approach the conversation with Lou, but not tonight. "Vin? What were you saying?"

The kitchen was clean, and he had set up a bed on the couch. Patagonia was curled up on his pillow, and Aristotle was stretched across a blanket, gently batting at her tail as she flicked it back and forth. She slowly blinked at him. Vin was at the window, looking out toward the Avenue with its glittering casinos.

The scene startled me with how homey it felt. I had this mental picture flash in my head of me walking over to him to watch the lights. He would slip an arm around me and pull me close.

He turned around to face me. "You going to just stand there?" He extended a sheet of paper.

I walked over to take it, avoiding looking at his face, as

I was sure the blush on my cheeks would give away my daydream from a moment ago. "What's this?"

"Instructions for how to dress tomorrow. We put together a plan after you left."

I scanned over the sheet and saw that it listed instructions for Golden Pyramid casino entry-level job requirements for day one. It included the directions for full makeup, absolutely no jewelry, and hair clean, dry, and pulled back into a bun. There were instructions on where to go and who to ask for. "What's the plan?"

"We have some information on where all the victims were in the days leading up to their death and narrowed down the list to a few best guesses that it looks like almost all of them were in according to the billing records. It's tough to say for sure because they could have used cash, but each of these places, most of the people visited, so we are starting with these. Mom had the idea that you should hang out in each location roughly around the time the victims did. You can see if any person, place, or thing grabs your attention. But since it would be obvious and odd to the employees if you stood around, we came up with this as an excuse for why you would be there."

"So you want me to work in each of these places? You want me to try to learn a new job while doing... What exactly am I doing to investigate? The same thing that I did today? Won't it be a bit obvious if I'm trying to learn a whole new job and trying—"

"Relax! Don't you think I have a plan?" His tone held more ire than seemed necessary.

I pursed my lips to keep from snapping back.

"The first place is the store. It's rather large and holds lots of miscellaneous items that people often forget like lighters, toothpaste, medicine, and tissues along with liquor, beer, water, and snacks, and the far end is a separate store that is more high-end. We'll spend some time in there, then we'll get into your job. Don't worry too much about what you're doing. You'll be a waitress, but mostly it consists of you standing around and looking pretty. You can manage that, can't you?" He sneered the question.

I wasn't sure if he was questioning my ability to look pretty or to stand around. I narrowed my eyes at him. "Hardly sounds like brain surgery. I think I can handle it." I turned to stomp off and immediately lurched forward, as Aristotle had been standing behind me. I tumbled over the large cat and barely broke my fall with my hands. The only saving grace was the couch blocking Vin's view. My hair had slid over my face, and my shirt had busted open. I flopped onto my side to fix my clothing, which was all askew, as if it had been hit by a tornado.

"You okay?"

I gritted my teeth at the tone of amusement in his voice. "Fine." Aristotle and Patagonia came to my face, and each one licked a cheek until I sat up. I couldn't bear to look at his face. My exit was ruined. "I'm going to bed!"

CHAPTER ELEVEN

I walked around the store and resisted the urge to smooth down my skirt. It was expensive and fit as well as it did when I bought it a half dozen years ago for a fancy New Year's Eve party. The black dress was nipped in at the waist, and the length revealed my shapely calves. I felt beautiful, and the casual glances as I had walked through the casino reinforced my opinion. Overall, I was feeling pretty good about myself.

Vin had requested that I put on something that screamed rich and cultured. I was sure he would be blown away by my appearance, but instead he had shrugged and said it was good enough.

I had been walking up and down the aisles of kitschy souvenirs as I relaxed and tried to be aware. The scant instruction Auntie Ann had given me when I arrived was that it was like what I did for reading an emotional hologram in that I needed to clear my mind and relax. Not a difficult task. She apologized for not being able to go with me, but she was helping Vanessa to sort through all the information they had on the victims.

The instructions didn't seem all that helpful until I tried it. Quickly, I could feel the emotions blooming around me like a subtle scent. Unlike the emotional holograms that were static and frozen, the current emotions around me ebbed and flowed as people's moods changed.

A group of girls in their twenties entered, and I drifted down the aisle toward them. They excitedly chatted, their makeup slightly smeared and their voices slurred from a night of drinking. They got armfuls of bottled water and snacks as they walked around in their bare feet and carried their heels. I got as close as I could, stared at the rows of diarrhea medicine, and tried to give the appearance of deep consideration as I listened to the gals chatter.

Their emotions spiked as they laughed about the evening. The lead girl, with her wife-to-be sash and her crown covered in tiny pink plastic penises, was overflowing with love. Tender affection for her friends surrounding her as well as her absent fiancé.

"Excuse me," a girl said while shoving me out of the way to reach for a gigantic bottle of pink medicine. Prickly irritation radiated off her as she unscrewed the bottle and took a generous gulp then pressed a hand to her stomach.

I drifted down the aisle toward an older couple picking through stuffed animals. Their deep love for each other filled my senses like a cool forest breeze.

I walked around the store, a bit confused about what I was doing here. I rounded a corner and ran into Vin, who was examining a display of snow globes. We had barely spoken today. Once we arrived, he had taken me to this store and immediately ditched me.

Unlike everyone else, I didn't immediately pick up anything from him. It wasn't just that he was relaxed with no strong emotions. It was as if they were hiding in a dark corner. I edged closer and pretended to examine the tiny replicas of the casino in the glass globes while I rummaged around to find Vin's emotions.

"Stop it." He growled, hints of irritation in his voice

and in the air.

"What?" I strove for innocent but knew I wasn't getting away with anything. I gave one last attempt to push past whatever was keeping me from reaching inside him.

He picked up a snow globe with two ceramic bunnies inside. The animals delicately touched noses while a red heart spun above their heads. The snow inside the globe was a mix of white, red, and pink hearts with glitter. It was small in his enormous hands.

"I would *not* have pegged you as the snow globe type."

"It reminds me of my great-great-grandmother." He turned and headed to the cashier while bouncing it in his hand.

"Wow. You knew her? I didn't even get to meet my grandparents. They passed before I was born."

He stopped and gave me a funny look before continuing toward the cashier. "She's still alive. Let's just say that longevity runs in my family."

I was tempted to ask more, but something in his tone warned me that now was not the time. I paused to consider the store. A glass wall separated the large store from a second, smaller store with more high-end items. The customers from earlier were all gone, but a new set of customers had wandered in. A man in expensive black pants wandered through the liquor section near a woman in a flirty and swishy dress of red, pinks, and purples. She excused herself as she passed in front of him, carrying a bottle of water. She got in line behind a man in a zoot suit.

I looked him over, as his outfit was unusual even in Rambler. The angular shoulders and pinstripes were reminiscent of Dick Tracy, both the comic strip and the campy movie.

I opened my senses and tried the read them from across the store. There was a mix of exhaustion and excitement in various amounts. The man in the zoot suit had a low simmering level of frustration, while the woman was feeling a different kind of frustration not rooted in anger. I struggled to get a handle on it until Vin got in line behind her and she turned to face him.

Her frustration was the sexual kind. She looked at him and batted her eyes at him, arching her back slightly to show off her décolletage. He nodded at her with a slight dip of his head, but his eyes remained blank. Her frustration flared as she turned to the cashier and slammed her water on the counter.

I went over to a display of candles and held one to my nose to hide my attempt to get a better, deeper reading. I breathed in the warm vanilla fragrance of the cream-colored candle as I closed my eyes. I searched and reached as far as I could through the store, but nothing stood out.

"Anything?" Vin's voice came from a few inches from my right ear, his breath tickling my skin.

I hid the chill that went down my spine with a shrug. "Nothing sinister, just people, though you disappointed that girl in line. She was giving you the eye."

He grunted and switched the paper bag with the snow globe into his left hand and placed the right one on the base of my back to direct me toward the glass doors of the high-end store. "Let's go in there." He leaned in close again. "Be careful."

"Of what?"

He held open the door, and cool, lightly perfumed air rustled the loose hair around my face. "Lots of magic in here."

CHAPTER TWELVE

I stepped through, and the hairs on my arm gently rose. The air was electrified and carried energy. The lights were brighter. I pulled in a deep breath, feeling revitalized, as though I had just awoken from a refreshing nap and slipped into my favorite sweater. There were racks of clothing, purses, and belts along with rows of shoes, art, high-end cosmetics, and a huge display of pet supplies.

I drifted over to the racks of crystal-studded leashes, harnesses, and bowls. I had spoken to Patagonia, asking her to stay at the loft today. Vin said that if she showed up, we would deal with it. As I left, she had been curled up with Aristotle in the center of my bed.

The store was amazing. Each item called to me. I started to pull a purple leather cat harness off the rack, when Vin put his hand over mine and stopped me.

"Don't." His voice was quiet so as to not carry in the small store.

"But it's so beautiful." I drifted over to a rack of purses and picked up a blue one. There were heavy metal buckles on the plethora of pockets. The leather was soft and supple. I lifted it to my cheek and rubbed it while breathing in the rich aroma.

"Stop that," Vin hissed. He reached for the purse, but I danced back and clutched it to my chest.

"No, it's the most beautiful thing I have ever seen." A small part of my brain wondered when I started to care so much about purses.

Vin grabbed my arm and pulled me close. "It's the magic. Give it to me."

I tried to pull away, shielding the most perfect and wonderful purse in the world from him. "What's magic?"

"The store. It makes you want to buy things. You don't really want a two-thousand-dollar purse."

My jaw dropped, and I dropped the purse to my side in shock.

He let go of my arm. "I didn't realize you would be so susceptible. Put the purse down, and see what you can find."

The purse was heavy in my hand. The metal was cold and smooth. Was it really magic that made it seem so special? Was it possible that the feelings I had about the purse were all fake?

I turned the purse over in my hands. Vin didn't know what he was talking about. This was the best purse on earth, and it would be mine.

I ducked hard and spun away, running across the store. Vin's footsteps behind me were heavy as a few seconds later he stomped behind me. I squealed as I ran behind a display and searched for a place to hide.

"Ella!"

At the sound of his voice, I stuffed the purse under my shirt and faced him. "I'm going to buy it, and I don't care what you say."

"You're magic sick. We need to clear your head." Vin bore down on me like a freight train.

I ran again, dashing around a shoe display. "My head has never been clearer."

A man behind the counter caught my eye. He gave me a smile. "Does the lady want to buy the purse?"

"Yes!" I ran past the counter as Vin raced up behind me and wrapped his arms around my waist, pinning my hands in front of me.

"Brian, cut out the magic. We've told you that we don't allow this level." Vin growled. "Deep breaths, Ella." He twined his fingers through mine.

His thick fingers pressed into my hand brought me back to the moment, and I ceased breathing as the contact heated up.

"Breathe, Ella!"

I took a shuddering breath and my head cleared. Vin's spicy scent filled my lungs and pushed out any thoughts of the purse. The two-thousand-dollar purse. A two-thousand-dollar purse that I had said I wanted to buy! "I don't want the purse. I don't!"

Vin dropped his arms from around me. "Good. Keep breathing, and hand it over."

I shivered as the remnants of magic fell away. With a clear head, it was easy to feel the sickly sweet magic that had compelled me to want to buy the purse and everything else in the store. I lifted my shirt and handed Vin the purse while avoiding touching his fingers. The outline of where his body had been pressed against me burned.

Brian, the man behind the counter, shrugged. "Sorry, Vin. I guess I don't know my own strength. Or maybe your little female friend really did want the purse?" He raised an eyebrow at me.

I shook my head. "No." I took a deep breath and took the chance to see if I felt anything in the store. Everything was covered with sweet-and-sticky magic on it that compelled me to hold it. The buy-it-and-take-it-home energy, and underneath it was something sneaky and distasteful, like when someone made a racist joke or yelled at a puppy. Whatever magic was happening here, it wasn't evil like the curse on the horse or the murders but wasn't innocent either.

Vin and Brian were arguing in harsh whispers. Vin

slammed a hand onto the glass countertop, knocking over a display of rings inside. "If you don't get your act together, I'll—"

"You'll what? Tell me what you plan to do!" Anger rolled off of Brian, and the sickly magic oozed from him. He was definitely the source of all the magic. He opened his mouth and jabbed a finger in Vin's direction, when his head jerked to stare at something behind me.

I started to look behind me, when something hit me hard from behind. I took my momentum and rolled, kicking at whatever had attacked me.

I hit the display of pet supplies as a wave of anger and jealousy crashed into me. Scrambling backward, I got a display of purses between me and the lunatic and got my first good look at her as Vin grabbed her from behind and pinned her arms behind her back.

She was taller than me, svelte, and had large breasts. Ample cleavage was showing above her tank top. She flicked her head to the side to get her black hair out of her face. The two most noticeable features to me were her extreme beauty and the waves of emotions rolling off of her. Primarily anger but with a noticeable amount of pain underlain below.

Vin showed the most emotion I had seen as he roared at her. *"Tiffany, what's wrong with you?"*

"I knew there was another woman." She fought against him.

I slowly stood up as a soft, furry body pressed against the side of my leg. Patagonia was twining herself through my feet. With an insistent meow, she rubbed her nose against my hand then arched her body into my palm.

I scooped her up with shaky hands and held her to my chest. The magic and the attack combined had sapped my strength, but her firm, wiggly body pressed against me grounded me. She wiggled out of my arms onto her new favorite place, my shoulders. She reached across my face to grab a back paw and started chewing on her claws. The delicate fur on her hind leg tickled my nose, and I pulled it off my face before I sneezed.

Vin angrily spoke into Tiffany's ear. Her expression dropped, and her arms gave up their fight. He let her go.

A second furry body pressed against me, and Aristotle had appeared and rubbed against my leg on his way to Vin. Tiffany looked over and caught sight of the enormous black cat pressed up against me and Patagonia, and her eyes flashed.

Before Vin could grab her, she sprang at me, but this time I was better prepared. Magic flared up around us. I didn't know what it meant or what she might be trying to accomplish, but I could at least tell that she was trying to do something.

I gritted my teeth and dodged to the side. Instead of hitting me straight on, she winged me, throwing us in opposite directions. She crashed into a rack of ballet slippers covered in rhinestones, which showered down around her. I landed at the base of a leather jacket display that slowly tipped over me.

I frantically clawed at the jackets, getting tangled in the security cords that attached the jackets to the rack.

Tiffany's anger was building as she shouted, "I knew there was something suspicious when you cancelled our date, you jerk. But how stupid are you to bring your slut here?"

Vin didn't reply, just glaring while his anger ratcheted up.

"I saw you hugging her." She stabbed a finger in my direction.

Adrenaline coursed through my veins, and my breathing was labored as I freed myself from the jackets. I moved away from Tiffany as she screamed at Vin. Fear built in my chest. Her anger was taking on a magical hint that I didn't understand. Fear crawled up my throat and constricted it.

Time seemed to slow. I was horrified when fire

sprouted from my fingertips. Brian appeared in front of me with a large red fire extinguisher. Instantly, I was enveloped in a white cloud.

My head cleared as I fell backward and coughed to clear my lungs of the noxious fumes. White powder covered me and most of the store.

Vin held a sobbing Tiffany. He pulled her up to look her in the eye. "Stop! You are acting like a child." He slowly bit off each word as he glared at her.

Tears streamed down her face then her neck and over her breasts and disappeared beneath the tank top. Silent weeping shook her shoulders as she looked up into Vin's face. "You said you loved me." The anger was slowly being replaced by deep despair.

His nostrils flared, and his annoyance radiated from his lifted shoulders and narrowed eyes. "What does that have to do with anything?"

Brian tidied up the store but had come to a sudden stop when Tiffany had spoken. Half of the merchandise was covered in white dust, and only a couple of displays were still upright. He absently dusted off a few items, but his attention was focused on Vin and Tiffany.

Tiffany sniffed hard and dragged the back of her hand across her nose. "I see the connection between you. I can see it. You're connected, and it wasn't there before."

Vin blew out a disgusted sigh. "It is not what you think."

"Then what could it possibly be?" she screamed, and the anger started to build.

Brian grabbed an armful of dog collars and leashes. "Just tell her. If she can see it, then there is no point dismissing it."

Vin glared at him before turning back to Tiffany. "Mom and Olivia are mentoring her. I got caught up in the bonding ceremony. That's all."

She sniffed delicately, but a glimmer of hope softened her face. "Really? Why didn't I see it before?"

"It just happened. You recognize Patagonia." He let go of her arm to point at Patagonia, who was twining herself between my knees.

"Oh...I didn't recognize her." She looked me up and down with a smug smile. "Isn't she awfully old to bond and start her training?"

He still had a heavy dose of anger toward her and the whole situation.

She wilted under his glare and turned to me. "Sorry." She didn't sound sorry, more like a five-year-old being forced to apologize.

"You ever come at me like that again, you'll regret it." I slowly enunciated each word. Even the nicest boarding schools had bullies, and I had learned that if you didn't stand up to them right off the bat, it would be a long school year.

Patagonia hissed, mimicking my aggression. Standing up on her hind legs, she clawed at the air, hooking her talons, as a robber would wield a blade. Unlike in my youth, I was not alone.

A tight smile briefly appeared on Vin's face but disappeared in a moment. "Settle down, and wipe your face off."

I scurried over to a mirror at the far end of the store while Vin and Tiffany spoke in hushed tones. My face was dotted with white powder that only smeared when I dragged my hand across my face. My eyes were red, and they stung. Patagonia, and Aristotle at her side, were pristine, without even a single fleck of white blemish on their black coats.

I reached over to pet Patagonia. Aristotle pressed himself into my other hand, so I scratched behind his ears. Both cats slammed into the back of my legs and purred loudly. Brian was on the store phone, talking to someone quietly.

In the reflection of the mirror, I watched Vin and Tiffany exchange a kiss. She turned to leave, and he

smacked her on the butt.
them. She threw a fake scow
sauntered away.

I watched Vin watch her until he
direction and caught my eye in the mirro
Ella."

I leaned over to pet the cats to hide my burn
I hadn't intended for him to catch me watching
though why wouldn't I? The woman had attacked me
of nowhere, and I had set my hands on fire. I had every
right to watch my back.

But that wasn't why I had watched. I had wanted to see
what they were to each other. Lovers, it appeared. Not that
it was any of my business, and I certainly didn't care. I
could barely stand the man.

I threw back my shoulders and went up to Vin. "What
the—"

"Not now." He completely dismissed me and turned to
Brian. "I'm not done with you. Shut the store, and walk
away for the rest of the week. Next week, we'll have an
investigation into how long you have been running your
magic well over the acceptable levels."

Brian rolled his eyes, but the slight hike in his shoulder
level gave away the nervousness that sprang up at the word
investigation. "Come on, Vin. We all push it a bit. I just got
carried away today."

"Doesn't matter."

He sighed. "At least let me clean up before everything
gets ruined."

"Fine. Pull the blinds before you start cleaning up since
you clearly can't be discreet with your magic." He caught
my eye. "Let's go. It might take magic to get you
presentable." He exited the door of the store, and I
stormed through the store to try to catch up with him.

He had the bag with the snow globe in it. It seemed
like a lifetime since he bought it. Aristotle jogged next to
him as Vin left the high-end store and pushed through the

atagonia kept
causing me to

red at the large
sino, but when
startled or burst

n hard to fall into

low down a little.
ow."

nt," I hissed before
a few steps before
catching ...   with him.

Desire radiated from both of
l over her shoulder as
rked his head in my
"We need to go,
g cheeks.
them,
ut

He chuckled. "That's ...   ers."

"Bull honky. She attacked me, and I'd rather it not happen again. Though if I see her again, maybe I'll get the drop on her."

Vin stopped in front of the same elevator we had used all day yesterday to investigate and pressed the button.

"Aren't there any other elevators in the whole casino? This one's starting to freak me out."

"Sorry, it's the closest." The doors opened, and we stepped inside, the cats racing in ahead to sniff the floor. He ran an employee card through a slot and pressed the basement two floor button. After the door slid closed, he turned to me. "Investigating murder *is* creepy. And don't jump Tiffany. You'll see her again because you're going to be a VIP server during her show."

I reached over and slammed my palm on the emergency stop button. Our descent halted, but an incessant alarm started blaring.

Vin glared at me then waved a hand over the control panel, and the noise stopped. I was momentarily distracted by the small burst of magic I felt as he silenced the alarm, but I wouldn't be stopped.

"Why don't you warn me about these things ahead of

time?"

"It wasn't necessary; just do what I tell you."

Patagonia stretched up to dig her claws into my thigh as her tail whipped back and forth nervously. The anger was building in me and crawling up my throat. "Do what you tell me? I'm not a dog."

"You're an employee."

"Fine. Then I quit!" I started pressing buttons, willing the elevator back to the main floor. There were reasons I had taken the job, but none mattered right now.

"Stop. Stop." He swallowed hard and struggled to form the next sentence. "I'm... sorry. Okay. I should have warned you more carefully about the magic in the store."

My hand paused, hovering over the buttons. "Oh?"

"It might have... helped you... be more prepared." He groaned slightly as if the admission caused him physical pain. "Though I had no way of knowing that you would be so susceptible or that he was running so much juice through the store."

"Don't!" My voice screeched in the enclosed space. Patagonia yowled and stood on her back legs to dig her front claws into my stomach. I took a second to compose myself. "If you had warned me that the store had that kind of magic, the compulsion to buy, I could have told you that it was hitting me hard. If you had warned your little girlfriend about what I was doing, she might not have attacked me."

"I already apologized about the store. I won't say it again."

It had been a weak apology at best, but there was no use belaboring the point. "And Tiffany?"

"Unavoidable. She could be a suspect."

I gasped. "You think your girlfriend could be a killer, and yet you are still dating her?"

He shrugged. "She's not exactly safe. We all agreed not to tell anyone what we were doing."

"Except Tiffany and Brian from the store both know I

am in magic training. And Isadora from the restaurant knows I'm investigating, though she thinks it's financial. And doesn't everyone know that I am trying out a bunch of different jobs today? This is the worst-kept secret in town." I crossed my arms and stomped a foot.

Vin burst out laughing. "Good point. Keep an eye out for anything suspicious, and you'll be fine." He reached out and pressed the down button.

The elevator started to descend. I clenched my jaw and reached over to press the button again, but Vin grabbed my wrist.

His hot hand held my wrist firmly but painlessly. "Don't. It's not good for the elevator."

I jerked my hand back but couldn't move an inch until he deliberately released it. "Fine, but I'm not doing another thing until you answer some questions."

The door to the elevator opened to the second basement floor, one below the stables. It was an employee-only level used to change into uniforms, store their things in lockers, or clock into work. I had been here a few days ago to check in before they sent me to investigate the finances of the casino. So much had happened since that it felt like an eternity ago.

Vin rolled his eyes. "Fine." He marched over to an office and leaned in through the open door. "Hey Greg, I'm here with the new girl, but I need your office."

"Sure thing, boss." Greg exited the office and gave me a smile. He had helped me with paperwork on my first day of work. "Hey, Ella, didn't realize they were taking you from accounting to waitressing. Odd, but not my business. I'll be back in a bit to get you all set up. Do you want me to bring you back coffee?"

"Thank you. Yes, I take it with cream." Greg had been fun and put me at ease my first day. This time I picked up the cozy, warm vibration of magic around him. I went into the office and took the chair behind the desk, the power seat.

Vin closed the door behind him and sat. "I forgot that you already met Greg."

"And yet another person that is suspicious of this whole setup. You might as well buy me a bungling investigation T-shirt. In fact, you get one as well."

"Is that what you wanted to talk about?" Vin sat back and crossed his arms over his chest.

"No. Well… yes, a little. What is the goal here? I mean, we are trying to hide the investigation, but everyone and their mom knows that something is going on."

"How so?" He quirked an eyebrow in question.

"Isadora knows I am doing some investigation, though you said it was financial. Brian from the store and Tiffany both know I am a mage or witch or whatever you call it. And they both heard you say that you were there when I got Patagonia. What was Tiffany's question about a bond all about?" At the mention of Patagonia's name, she leapt onto my lap. Aristotle came to my side and started grooming her face.

"Tiffany can see how people are connected." He sat and stared at me, saying no more.

I sucked in a breath through my teeth as agitation rose in my chest. "I swear! If you don't start answering my questions, I *will* leave."

"I answered."

"Then use more words. Lots of words. Tell me something useful, you big lump of muscle."

The corners of his mouth subtly lifted. "Okay, I'll try."

I blew out a breath and started over. "What is the bond that she was talking about, and I guess she could see it because of magic?"

"Yes." He nodded and put an ankle on the knee of the other leg and leaned back. "She specializes in seeing how people are connected and can affect some of those connections. Her show is billed as 'for lovers,' so it makes sense. She could see a connection between us." He avoided my eyes at the end, broadcasting his unease.

"What bond is that? She thought we were... a thing." I twisted up my mouth in disgust at having to say it out loud.

"I was one of the three witnesses when the familiar bond between you and Patagonia was forged. Normally, that is done by family members and mentors, people that have a significant relationship. I didn't want to get mixed up in it, but there was no one else present. Mom said I could stay out of it, but apparently the magic felt differently. Now we are working together, and it is getting stronger."

I gasped and looked between us, half expecting to see a physical rope between us. "No, eww, I don't want to be tied to you."

"Neither do I! But magic doesn't care. Once we catch the mage behind the murders, we can stop working together, and the bond will fade. That's how these things work."

"Couldn't she see that it wasn't romantic then?"

"No, bonds aren't really color coded by activity. She probably could tell it was positive but not the exact nature, and when combined with me holding you, she just jumped to conclusions."

"Why did you hold me like that?"

"To help ground you and break the magic. I thought you were stronger than that, though I didn't realize how much power he was pumping into that store." He checked his watch.

"Don't even think about it. I'm not done."

"Then what do you want to know?" He flexed his head side to side then grabbed the top of his head and his chin and, with a violent jerk, popped his neck. It sounded like a symphony of walnuts being busted open.

I cringed. "Two questions. First, isn't my cover totally blown? Shouldn't we cancel?"

"And do what instead? Just let someone else die? That is why I am shadowing you today. Tiffany loves to gossip.

The news is probably already getting around that we're sponsoring your training. It's not uncommon for a sponsoring family to find a job for the apprentice. Plus, Olivia owns the casino. She gets to do what she wants."

I tapped my front teeth. "What am I doing for the rest of the day? And please warn me ahead of time about any potential problems."

"You are going to be a waitress in three different locations: the high-end gambling tables, Isadora's Ristorante, and the show that Tiffany does. The same group of waitresses float between these locations, so it isn't that weird that you would appear in each place throughout the day. Mostly, girls stick to one area, but trying out different places isn't unusual when you start."

"How am I supposed to get a reading on the place while running around working?"

"You only get drinks and maybe some light food. But like I said, the waitresses stand around and look pretty. You'll need to shower first, but I think you can handle that." He broke into a big smile.

I tipped my head to the side then looked down. I had forgotten that I was covered head to toe in the fire extinguisher foam. I chuckled and kicked a foot to spin the chair. "Stand around and look pretty. Got it. What else? Won't other mages think it is weird that I'm a waitress? I mean if they can tell?"

"Everyone that's a mage here probably already knows. That's gossip for you. But they won't think it's weird. All the high-end waitresses are mages."

I slammed my feet on the floor mid spin to stare at him. "What? Why?"

"One of the best-paying jobs in the place. The tips alone are more than you would have made as a freelance employee. Plus they are part of what makes this place so successful. They are part of every aspect of the hotel and can influence our guests to have the best experience possible. Other casinos are starting to copy us, but our casinos are so far ahead." He sat back with a smug smile.

"Casinos? Plural?"

He nodded. "The family has a variety of investments; between our family and Olivia, we own a good chunk of Rambler."

"Wow." I would need to do some online searching to confirm the statement since I was not one to believe someone just because they said so. But I could also sense his confidence in the statement. He believed himself—that much was true. "You must have an advantage being able to use magic and running casinos."

His eyebrows knitted. "What do you mean? Everyone powerful in Rambler's a mage."

My eyebrows flew up in response. "Seriously?"

He laughed and put both feet on the floor. "Of course. The mob ran Vegas. The mages run Rambler. But enough of a history lesson." He stood up.

Patagonia leapt off my lap. "Wait, what about the cats?"

He opened the door as the cats bounded out and shrugged at me. "You can ask them to go home, but if they want to come, there is nothing we can do. Let's find Greg and get you ready for work."

CHAPTER THIRTEEN

I turned around in front of the mirror, inspecting my waitress uniform. "No, no, no, no."

Greg leaned against the table in the small fitting room. "What's wrong? It fits perfectly. Normally we have a gal that helps you get fitted, but I think I did a pretty good job."

I turned my back to the mirror and looked over my shoulder. "My butt's hanging out."

"How else would people see the adorable gold panties? All the elite waitresses wear this. What size shoe are you?" He turned to a wall of high-heeled shoes.

"Eight. This can't be the way it is supposed to fit." The uniform consisted of a white dress with gold trim. It reminded me of what I had seen in hieroglyphs in college textbooks. It had a square neckline that showed all the cleavage I had and was formfitting down to the gold-trimmed hem that landed several inches shy of hiding the shiny gold panties. I had left all my jewelry at home, and there was nowhere on my outfit for my channeling stone. I felt magically naked along with physically.

"Put these on." Greg handed me the kitten heels with tiny gold buckles and threw open the door to the room.

I sat in a chair to put on the shoes and was thankful that I had carefully shaved my legs last night. Toe hair would not have completed the look.

Vin leaned in the door. "You ready? Whoa." He pulled his head back. "That is a lot of hair."

I had to wash my hair after the fire extinguisher, and thankfully the nice locker room had a set of showers with soap, shampoo, and conditioner. They even had hairdryers. My hair was loose around me. It fell in waves to my butt and was a natural red that others paid for. It was my pride and joy.

I pushed it out of my eye. "Yes." I smiled at him. Men loved my hair loose, but I kept it back in a bun most times. He was probably going to compliment it, and I loved the compliments. Men and women would stop me to comment on it when it was down, comparing it to flames or even *The Little Mermaid*. It was my personal vanity.

"It looks like... uh..." He stuttered to find the right word. "You know, one of those polygamists! A sister wife."

I groaned. "Seriously?" It was rude and dismissive of him after a long morning of being a pain in the butt. Though he had finally answered a few questions, that didn't change the fact that talking to him was difficult and getting him to be forthright was like pulling teeth from a cranky tiger. His mouth was still moving.

"I prefer short hair, but I guess if you had a hair fetish, it would be cool." His voiced faded out as I glared. You'd think he'd know how to at least pretend to be polite. Clearly his overdeveloped muscles left no blood to circulate to his pea brain. It took me a second to recognize he was asking a question. "You ready or what?"

I glared at him. "Where do I put my stuff?" I gestured to an oversized purse I had brought with makeup and hair supplies. I dug out a clip and flipped my head over to twist my hair into a bun that I secured with the clip.

"Here." Greg grabbed the bag and went through a

door then returned with a key. "Here. There's a safety pin to secure inside your brassiere. Have fun!"

I secured the key then trotted into the hallway toward the elevator. Tapping my foot as I stood next to Vin, I avoided eye contact then rushed in when the doors opened.

Vin followed and pressed a button as the two cats darted through the closing doors and chased each other around the elevator.

Reflected in the polished chrome trim, Vin opened his mouth then closed it without saying anything as we rose until the elevator lurched to a stop. "Patagonia, Aristotle, go home."

The doors opened to the floor above the main casino floor. Though it was similarly appointed in an ancient Egyptian theme, here, everything felt a bit nicer. The carpet was brighter, cleaner, and was more comfortable underfoot. The metal surfaces were smoother and held a better polish. The tiles that designated the walkways shone like glass and appeared to be a natural stone.

My kitten heels clicked along, and a quick glance at my ankles revealed that the two black cats had disappeared. I suddenly felt far more alone, even as crowds of people pressed around the tables.

"I'll get you checked in, then you can start reading the room. I'll stay to keep an eye out for you but I'll be at the back of the room."

Without making eye contact, I nodded. "Okay." My voice was harsher than I expected.

"Are you pissed again? What did I do this... Oh! This is because I didn't fawn all over your pretty red hair." Amusement rolled off him.

"What! No. I just... You were really rude!" The room was filled with the noise of hundred-dollar slots singing their song of bells and whistles, and cheers from the various tables of craps and roulette. The lower tables were five-hundred-dollar minimum and went up from there.

He smirked. "You're mad because I didn't compliment you. You're used to every man falling all over you because you're beautiful. You expect them—"

"You think I'm beautiful?" The words tumbled out in shock.

His stride faltered ever so slightly.

My cheeks flared red, and I changed the subject. "Everyone played here?" I used a stage whisper that would hopefully carry to only his ears.

"Yes." He cut across the room toward a wall and stopped a dozen feet from a bar. He looked around for anyone within eavesdropping distance before continuing. "Victim one, Michael, often came here when he worked in his mother's restaurant. Joe, the poker player, was in a tournament over there."

He pointed to a glass-enclosed room with serious players around tables.

"Roberta, who was here with a convention, came with some friends. She didn't gamble or stay long. Tony was a blackjack dealer here in the room, and Ethel won a couple thousand at a slot machine and came up here right before she died. They were all here at some point."

A waitress in the same outfit as me came by. "Hey, Vin, you working today?"

"Hey, Natasha. Yep, some security. Can you grab Ella here a Shirley Temple, extra syrup, please?"

She smiled at me, and I was dazzled by her white teeth and clear eyes. Instantly, I wanted to be her best friend, and all the tension in my neck disappeared.

She turned to me. "Hi, Ella. We're going to work together today. I'll be right back with your drink." She left and headed for the bar.

"Did you feel that?" Vin leaned over to whisper.

I was still staring at her, wondering if I had ever met anyone nicer. "What?"

"She turned on the charm. That was her magic, or some of it, at least."

"Oh! She's really good. I wanted to be her new best friend forever."

"You should. She's really nice and very talented. But you need to pay better attention. When suddenly you have overwhelming emotions like that, you need to assume something magical is happening. I'll tell Mom to help you with some mental boundaries as soon as possible, but for now, just be suspicious."

"Why did you order me a Shirley Temple? I'm not five." I took a few deep breaths and started looking around the room, seeing what I could pick up. As soon as I paid attention, there was a muffled dull sensation.

"Sugar. I don't carry a purse full of candy like my mom. You're going to shadow Natasha until you get enough of an idea of the job to fake it on your own. Try not to do too much reading around her. She'll know what you are doing. She's very good."

"If I was pretty and talented like her, I'd do something more interesting than waitressing, regardless of the pay."

"Don't you worry about her. She's just doing this between jobs. She was the wacky neighbor on some sitcom that was just cancelled. Her family owns a couple of casinos, but she said she prefers to be out from under their heel."

I squinted my eyes at her before turning back to Vin. When I pictured her with a crazy haircut, an oversized floral jacket, hunched over, and wearing heavy-framed glasses, I could hear her catchphrase from the television show, which had been on every Thursday. "'I'm gonna have a cow!'"

Melodic laughter sounded behind me, and Natasha came around to hand me a drink. "That's me. It was such a fun show, but the LA traffic is brutal. Got a place at the beach, thinking I would spend my evenings digging my toes into the sand and watching the sunset, but instead it was a place I crashed for a few hours in the dark. If there was an accident on any freeway, I would just get a hotel room near the studio. Are you new to town?"

"Uh." I was star struck, and it took a few beats for my brain to catch up. "Sort of. Been here for a bit but haven't really got out much. I—"

"Ella?" Vin raised an eyebrow.

"Oh. I should get to work."

Natasha flashed her perfectly shaped white teeth in another smile. "Of course. Did they tell you to keep an eye out for physical magic? Security has an eye out all the time, and there is the magic buffer you can feel that tamps down the cheating, but the hustlers are always trying something new."

"Physical magic?"

"Yeah, pushing on the roulette ball or nudging the dice at the craps table. But don't worry. A little charming magic is allowed except in the poker room, but they have normal waitresses." She crinkled up her nose. "The poker room is a total dead zone for magic. So gross. Anyways, I'll show you how to take orders and get them from the bar. This job is super easy. Come on. Tips are waiting."

Vin put a hand on my shoulder and leaned over. "If you see anything, let me know. I'll be in the corner."

CHAPTER FOURTEEN

Time flew as I raced around the floor, first tailing Natasha to learn the job then on my own. She was right. The job was pretty straightforward, plus it wasn't too crowded. We were the only two waitresses, and I had offered to take the half of the room farthest from the bar so I had an excuse to canvas the whole room and see what I could find.

She had encouraged me to keep moving. Otherwise, I was a target for drunk men looking to take home more than just some winnings. The balls of my feet had gone numb from the heels and constantly walking, but still I hadn't found anything to point to the killer.

The atmosphere of the room varied from table to table and over time. The craps table at one point had a great run of luck. The cheering and excitement rolling off the table was strong enough to make me feel drunk when I went by too closely. The poker room, on the other hand, was deadened from the magic, and I stifled a yawn as I passed to deliver a tray of drinks to a blackjack table.

The lack of magic meant that all the emotions I felt were also gone. It was quiet and calm, and I instantly wanted to take a nap. But once I moved past the poker room, energy of the gamblers filled me. I caught Vin's eye, and he jerked his head, indicating I should come over.

I nodded in return, showing that I would go over as soon as I was done. The drinks were complimentary to the gamblers as the casino wanted to keep everyone in good spirits of all kinds. As I delivered the orders to the customers, they slipped chips onto my tray. I scooped up a variety of ten-dollar— and even one fifty-dollar—chips into the attached purse that pulled down under the weight of my tips. I'd emptied the pouch once already since I had started the shift. The tips would quickly outpace the fee they were paying me for my part of the investigation.

I weaved through the tables toward Vin, doing one last reading. The general room had peaks and lows of emotions like anticipation, excitement, joy, and frustration, but one roulette table felt different. There was a buzz that I couldn't place, like the noise of a high-voltage power line, while whispers of fear were tinting the edge of the investigation.

As I passed the roulette table, an older gentleman leaned back in his chair. "Pardon me, miss." His grey felt cowboy hat matched his grey handlebar mustache perfectly.

"Yes, sir?" I halted and gave him a big smile.

His energy was warm and woodsy, as I had always imagined a grandfather should have. It reminded me of smoke from an old-fashioned pipe. Unlike so many men in the room, his eyes never strayed from my face. "I'd like to get a beer for me and my wife."

He gestured to his side, where a lovely older woman's eyes were glued to the table in front of her. Her slender fingers flipped a hundred-dollar chip across the back of her finger. When her husband nudged her, she turned to face him, and the crow's feet at each eye crinkled as she smiled at him with her whole face.

Their love was apparent and basked me in the warm emotion. Instantly, I was hit with a wave of sadness of my own that I had no one that looked at me that way or made me feel the love that radiated off them. Just as quickly, I shoved down my jealousy and tried to just enjoy the way it felt to be in their presence. I listed off the beers we had while only sneaking a few glances at the cheat sheet on my tray and took their order.

I was turning to leave when the woman's cool hand gently brushed my forearm. Her smooth fingertips sent a vibration of magic up my arm that was cool and crisp like inhaling wintergreen. "Dear, I have a vision for you." Her voice was a whisper that cut through the noise around us.

She closed her eyes and breathed deeply, the magic around her gathering like storm clouds rolling in from the ocean. When they reopened, they were all white, even the irises and pupils, though the weight of her stare pinned me in place.

"The bear and badger you seek will find you. Trust them." She lowered her head and blinked hard. When her gaze returned to my face, her irises were back to a watery blue, and the pupils dilated before returning to a normal size. She smiled.

My breath caught in my throat. Bear and Badger were the names of the men that my father had mentioned in the note. The ones that were supposed to train me. Though I hadn't started my search, I had thought of them often and tried to formulate a plan on how to search for them once we found the killer and my time was my own again.

"Where are they? Where should I look? What do you know?" The questions fell out of my mouth quickly, one after another.

She waved a hand. "Oh, I don't understand the messages. I just pass them on. Can I get a lime for my beer?" She squeezed my forearm and turned back to the table to spread chips over it for the next roll of the roulette wheel.

I stepped back on shaky feet, adrenaline coursing through my veins. I gulped then raced over to Vin, twisting my ankle a little as I tripped over my feet.

"What happened? Is the murderer here?" Vin reached

out and grabbed my arms to steady me as I stumbled. He looked over my shoulder, eyes narrowed and scanning the crowd.

"No... Maybe... I don't know." I gulped and swallowed hard. Could they be involved in the deaths? I had felt love from them then a surge of magic. It was scary and intimidating but nothing evil or dark. Though there was something in the room. "Hold on."

I scanned and was able to identify a growing emotion of anxiety that emanated from the roulette table. "Who are the older couple at that roulette table, the third table from the end?

"Oh!" he said with deep understanding. "Did one of them give you a prediction?"

I nodded.

He dropped his arms. "That can be unsettling. They're our seers, Gertrude and Ralph. They're married and work for the casino. They're excellent advisors all the time and often have predictions. The visions aren't predictable and are not always what we want to know, but they end up being what we need to know."

"She said—"

"No," he cut me off. "Don't tell me. You need to start training, or you're really going to step in it. Never tell someone a vision meant for only you. If you do, things get weird."

"Weird how?"

"Just weird, and I don't want to be all mixed up in it. Unless it has to do with— Never mind. I don't want to know regardless."

"Could they be mixed up in the murders?" I cast a furtive glance over my shoulder.

"Possible but unlikely, at least not them. They do what they want, how they want, and they know enough of the future that we never would suspect them if it was them."

"And we don't suspect them, so maybe they're the ideal suspects." The adrenaline was wearing off, and I was safe by Vin's side, so I no longer shook.

"Why do you suspect them at all?"

I turned to face the table. "Something's going on over there."

"What?" He looked over to a far corner and signaled a large security man over.

"I'm not sure." I bit my lower lip as I tried to find the words to describe it.

"That's super helpful." He stepped over and whispered to the man before returning. "He's going to check things. Can you try to describe what you're sensing?"

I scrunched up my face. There was anticipation, anxiety, and a hint of naughtiness. I relaxed and tried to let the word I was looking for come to mind. When it did, I opened my eyes. "Sneaky. It feels sneaky."

"Evil? Like that curse on the horse. Is that what you mean?"

"No, not like that at all. It's a new feeling. Someone is up to something, but it doesn't... I don't know, but it definitely feels sneaky."

He blew out a sigh and mumbled under his breath, "Amateur."

"I heard that."

"You were supposed to. Go find an excuse to go over there and see if you can't nail it down a bit more."

I spun away and glided over to the bar to pick up the beers the seers had ordered. Gertrude and Ralph. What kind of names were those for people who could see into the future? And the information she had given me was helpful, even hopeful. I had been so focused on this investigation that I hadn't had time to think about what to do next. Had my dad left more clues? Why had he been so secretive? Why hadn't he told me about his and my abilities?

Maybe it wasn't that I had been so busy. Maybe it was that I wasn't ready to unpack all my emotions about his death by investigating his life. Losing him had devastated me and left me an orphan in a cruel world. I sniffed away a tear and pushed away the thoughts. If I thought any more about his loss in my life, I would break down crying.

The bartender pushed over the two beers along with a lime in a shot glass that I moved to my tray. Slapping a smile on my face, I turned to deliver them and immediately stumbled over a furry body. Once I regained my balance, tray still full, I stared down at Patagonia.

"Shoo. Not now."

She blinked at me before bending over to gnaw at the tiny gold buckle on my shoe.

I looked for Vin and pointed at Patagonia.

He shrugged and gestured toward the roulette table. Cat or no cat, I had a job to do.

I shook Patagonia off my shoe and strode across the room, eyes darting to take in everything while I paid attention to all the emotions.

As I approached the table, I slowed down and was able to slowly trace the emotions back to the source, like sniffing out a hidden smell. The reason I had struggled before became apparent when I realized the emotions were emanating from three men spaced evenly around the table. They all had the same sneaky feeling—a mix of anticipation, anxiety, and devious intentions. I would need to get closer and see if I could figure out more.

I lifted a drink and stepped toward Gertrude to hand her the beer, when suddenly I was hurtling forward, my foot caught on something. The tray slid forward and crashed through the space between the two seers and landed among the piles of chips comprising the bets for this spin.

The beer in my right hand flew out and landed in the roulette wheel as it spun. A spray of beer flung out in a circle, spraying everywhere and everyone.

I fell, twisting around to avoiding hitting anyone, and my momentum rolled me across the floor. When I stopped rolling, Patagonia raced to my face to lick the beer off my nose then gently bat at my ear.

I took a few deep breaths as the rest of the casino erupted into noise, but even above the din, something had changed. I ran a hand over my limbs and pressed my outfit down to cover as much of my body as it could as I got up. I had carpet burns on one knee and elbow that were already stinging, and my back was feeling dodgy, but that wasn't all.

The people at the roulette table were shouting or wiping beer off their clothing. Or at least most of them were. What was missing was the sneaky emotion I had been feeling and the three men at the table. There were three noticeably empty chairs, one right where I had tripped. He had stuck out his foot to trip me!

Vin was running up to the table, his entire face a mask of anger.

"Vin, those guys." I jabbed at the empty chairs, my voice breaking in excitement.

He slowed up, and the anger transformed to confusion. "Who?"

I grabbed his arm and pressed myself up against him to talk into his ear. "The thing I was feeling was from those three guys, but they're gone. I think one of them tripped me." The words were all jammed together into one long string of sounds. I pressed a hand to my bun, which was sloppily hanging over one ear and starting to unravel.

He caught the eye of a security guard hovering near the table and jerked his head then turned to me. "Are you sure? From where I stood, it looked like you tripped over that piece of carpeting that came loose."

A corner of the luxe carpet poked into the air. The errant fabric stuck up in approximately the same place I had tripped, and it would make the most sense for what had happened, but I was quite sure that it wasn't the culprit. Something firm had caught my ankle, perhaps a shoe or shinbone, plus the flare of emotions that rose as I fell were definitely connected. The fact that the three men were now missing sealed the deal. I nodded. "That is definitely what I experienced. Maybe magic was involved to make me feel something else..." I trailed off at the end. What did I know about magic?

Vin looked me in the eyes and seemed to be weighing my words against what he had seen. After a moment, he nodded and turned to the security guard that had come to his side. "There were three men here at the roulette table that are now gone. Find them and detain them. I'm going to do an interrogation."

Half the security team raced from the room. Vin turned to me. "Wait here. I'll send someone down to take you to the next assignment." He didn't bother to get my agreement before leaving.

The other half of the security team started gently clearing the room of gamblers. They offered to make reservations for them at restaurants, provide a personal shopper at one of the many stores, or even find tickets to sold-out shows later in the day. Anything to keep them happy.

Gertrude and Ralph slowed in front of me. This time I could see they had matching rhinestone boots and belts, giving them an upscale cowboy look.

Gertrude patted my arm. "Don't worry, honey. I stumble over things too."

Ralph laughed loudly and gave his bride a hearty kiss on the cheek. "You always have been a bit clumsy, but you're as beautiful as the day we met." He patted my shoulder with one wrinkled and veiny hand. "You are more powerful than you know, even without training."

My eyebrows shot up. There had been no surge of magic power around him. "Is that a vision?"

He barked with laughter before breaking into a phlegmy cough. "No, not this time. I can see that with my own eyes. You can take care of yourself, sweetie. Don't forget that."

CHAPTER FIFTEEN

Natasha kept me company as the staff cleared the entire high-end gambling room. She had assured me not to be embarrassed and said that a few weeks ago she had also tripped over a piece of carpeting and spilled an expensive drink on the mayor.

The conversation had gradually drifted to local restaurants and her life on the sitcom show. We were making loose plans to grab a meal together in the future, my first real plans since I'd moved to the city, when Vanessa joined us in a waitress outfit.

"Hey, Natasha. Picked out your next big acting gig yet?"

"Not yet. Still figuring out my goals. I'm going to take off. My shift's been over for twenty minutes. Ella, I'm serious. You, me, fondue, soon."

"Absolutely. Looking forward to it." Once Natasha was out of earshot, I leaned over to Vanessa. "What's going on with the outfit?"

She bounced on her toes and spun in a circle. "Doesn't it look great? This is going to be so fun."

"What is?" I reached over to pet Patagonia, who had just woken up from a nap.

"I'm going to be your investigating partner. We can go undercover together." She squealed and reached down to scoop Patagonia into her arms. She scratched the black fur covering Patagonia's belly until the cat bit into her hand and yowled in displeasure. Vanessa danced over to a craps table and dumped the cat onto the felt.

"I'm not sure she is supposed to be up there."

Patagonia pounced on a set of dice and flipped them across the table then chased after them to repeat the game.

"She's fine. Who's going to tell *me* what to do? I practically own the place. I mean, not me, but the family. Anyways, there are people to fix it. That's their job." She was far more animated than I had seen her before.

Patagonia jumped off the table and meowed at my side. "Is Vin coming back?"

She rolled her eyes at the mention of her brother. "No, he's interrogating some dudes and needed someone to go with you to the Ristorante. Come on. Let's head down there."

We exited the room past posted security guards and pressed the button on the elevator. "He's not, like, magically breaking anyone's kneecaps, is he?" A chill went down my spine. If anything like that was involved, I was ready to skedaddle.

"Of course not. He knows when someone is lying. That's why he's in security. He'll get to the bottom of it then drop them outside of town." She entered the elevator as the doors opened, and pressed the button before spinning around to check her reflection in the shiny metal inside.

"Why not the police?"

"Eww. You don't turn mages over to human police. They'll be banned from town if they're guilty. That's enough. Unless they, like, kill someone."

The elevator doors opened, and I snapped my fingers to get Patagonia's attention before we exited. "And if they do, like, kill someone?" I strode purposefully toward the restaurant, trying to avoid the glances of gamblers hoping to order a drink.

"We call the Federal Order, and they take care of it. Hey, so what are we doing in the Ristorante? Like, what's our mission?"

I stumbled in shock. "You don't know? Didn't Vin tell you what the plan is? All I know is that we are going to Isadora's Ristorante."

"Oh, yeah, I just left so quickly that he probably forgot to tell me. Hold on. I'll call and find out." She raced over to a nook and picked up a white phone with no dial pad. She held it between her left ear and shoulder. She tapped a foot and started snapping the fingers on her right hand, creating a little flash.

I moved in closer, sure that my eyes were deceiving me, but they weren't. On each snap of her fingers, a little flame burst into life and danced on the tip of her fingers before slowly extinguishing.

I had made fire but only when being attacked by a jealous girlfriend or having a gun pulled on me by a madman. She was forming it while casually talking on the phone. It didn't even seem that she was fully aware of what she was doing. Was that how causally mages could handle magic? Could I do that once I had practice?

She hung up the phone and came over. "I've got the plan. We're—"

"Can you make fire just by snapping your fingers?"

Her cheeks flushed a little. "I didn't realize I was doing it again. It's a nervous tic, but Mom doesn't want me doing it in public. I thought I had broken the habit." She giggled.

"That's amazing! Can all mages do it?"

She smiled broadly and puffed up a little. "If they train hard enough and have the natural talent, then yes, but I wouldn't call it easy. But I can teach you. I'm sure you have the talent to do it." She grabbed my arm. "I'm so excited to have someone else to train with. Mom said we can start next week."

"What? Don't you already have your training?" This was news to me.

She struck a falsetto and held up a hand that she moved like a puppet as she talked. "A true mage is *never* done training." Rolling her eyes, she snapped her fingers, and a little yellow flame sparked into life again. "Or at least that is what my mom is constantly harping at me. I love her, I really do, but I just want to have fun. Is your mom like that?"

"Uh..." My mother, our relationship, and whatever happened to her so many years ago was not something I was ready to blurt out. Luckily, the question appeared to be hypothetical.

"They treat me like a baby. I'm a grown woman, and I want to start finding my own destiny, not just following Mom around the world, teaching rich, spoiled mages. Now that we're settled here, I thought that I could have a real life, but instead I get to play secretary and study even more. Potions, spells, protections, talismans—"

"So all that stuff is real?" There was so much to learn.

"Totally. Basically, most of the stuff you see in movies and TV or read in books is kinda true, but they also get it wrong. But it is so boring to study it. I want to *do* things. But finally, something interesting's happening." She squealed and did a little dance in her gold heels.

I would consider murders scary, not interesting, but to each their own. Speaking of which, it was time to get back on track. "Did you learn the plan?"

Her eyebrows flew up as she remembered. "Yes, totally. We're not actually working in Isadora's Ristorante, which makes sense since this is a bit much for a classy restaurant." She gestured down at her outfit and laughed. "No, we're working in the betting lounge. They serve appetizers and desserts from Isadora's. The chocolate cakes are delicious and have a special ability."

At the mention of chocolate cake, my stomach grumbled. "What kind of ability can a cake have? Water skiing?"

"Beth's the pastry chef and a mage that specializes in emotions. She has a special series of flavored chocolate cakes for different things like lust, happiness, and motivation. They're a hundred and fifty dollars a slice but super effective. My mom keeps buying me slices of motivational mint mocha, hoping that I will get serious with my studies. They help, but mostly I just get antsy to find a purpose in my life."

"I'm sorry." I had been jobless for a few years, rattling around my father's loft without a purpose. I was the last person to have advice for her.

Patagonia meowed and scratched at my calf. Several tourists were taking their picture with a cell phone and looked ready to approach.

I grabbed Vanessa and dragged her in the direction of the Ristorante. "I thought I was looking into the Ristorante, not some gaming room."

"You were until I did some more digging. They all had charges to the Ristorante, but when I reviewed, I noticed that there was a weird asterisk next to Isadora's Ristorante. It bugged me, so I went back to check, and sure enough, the asterisks meant that while the charge went to there, the order originated in the betting lounge." She smirked at her own brilliance.

"Great catch. That's a lot like what I do in my financial audits. Tell me about the betting lounge."

"Just a huge room with like a million televisions playing games and races from all over the world. It is one of the only places in the casino with really good Wi-Fi and cell reception so people can research their bets. They have to be betting or eating. Otherwise, security uses a spell to make their chairs super uncomfortable." She snickered. "But only the humans can bet here. The rest have to call their bets into Vegas, if a bookie will even take them. This way." She pulled me past the front of the Ristorante toward the huge gold door.

"Mages aren't allowed to gamble? I thought upstairs—"

"No, no, they can gamble at things like craps, roulette, slot machines, or card games. We have spells and security to enforce that they don't mess with those. But betting on things outside our control? No way. There isn't a way for us to make sure that all boxing matches, horse races, elections, and stuff weren't meddled with. That would be a lot of magic to use just to win a bet, but we don't risk it. That's part of the reason that mages like it here. In Vegas, they could gamble and even cheat, but then they get picked up by security for being too lucky, and it's a whole scene. There are some that still prefer Vegas, but most mages know that Rambler is where you come to have a good time." She pulled open the gold door, and we stepped inside.

The room was enormous, and she hadn't been exaggerating about the television sets. They were four high and ran the entire length of the back, one full side wall, and half of the other side wall of the room. The only wall not covered was the side that faced into the casino, and instead, that wall was solid windows to entice people in. On the closest side to the televisions were tables with piles of magazines and newspapers. The center of the room had a more casual setting, comfortable chairs gathered around tables.

Some of the people had on headphones, and each television had a large number pinned to the corner. The half of the side wall that wasn't covered in live footage of various events instead had two kiosks, one marked House Bets and the other Off-Site Bets. Tucked in between was a door where a waitress exited, carrying a tray of drinks and a bowl of ice cream.

I followed Vanessa as she weaved through the crowd, her hips swaying significantly more as heads swiveled to watch her movement. A few heads might have swung my way as well, but my hips were locked as I marched behind her and followed her through the door.

After passing through the door, we followed a wide hallway into a kitchen through two swinging doors. It was bustling with activity as people moved to a window to call out orders or pick up plates to put onto trays and race out through another set of doors.

"Are you Ella?"

I turned to my right, where a petite brunette with her hair pulled into a tight bun stood waiting. She wore a stiff white jacket, white pants, and bright-pink leather clogs.

"Yes, and this is Vanessa. She will also work."

"Fine, fine. I'm Beth. I make all the desserts. I don't mean to be rude, but I really need to get back to work. The menus are here. Put in your orders at the window. Those orders take about ten minutes since they are appetizers, so go and get more orders before picking them up. That goes for everything except the special chocolate cakes, the hundred-and-fifty-dollar ones. I need those orders personally. Go to that window"—she gestured to a small additional window along a different wall than the main ordering window—"and ring the bell." She leaned in close and whispered, "I need to spell those special. After you give me the order, please wait until it's ready, and deliver it right away so the magic is strong."

She disappeared back through the door, leaving us to grab trays and menus and formulate a good game plan for faking the next few hours.

And fake it we did. Most of the people already had food and drinks, and only the occasional new customer came in. It was a more relaxed environment than the energy of the high-value craps tables before. The room held the same emotions floating around but to a more relaxed degree. In fact, it was so laid back that I was starting to feel sleepy.

Patagonia had found a chair and curled up. Her nose was tucked under a back leg, giving her the appearance of a fuzzy black pillow. I kept one eye on her and stopped to pet her a few times.

Vanessa came over and flopped into the chair next to Patagonia and reached over to pet her fuzzy rump. "Dude, I've gotten so many tips. Having a job is awesome."

"You've never had a job?" I scanned the room as we talked in case anyone needed to place an order.

"Nope, never. Studying is my job but not for much longer. You figure out anything?"

I shook my head and held up a finger to wait to a young blond woman with barely any clothing who gestured. "Not a thing. I think this is a dud. How long are we supposed to stay? Anything special I am supposed to keep an eye on? Is Vin coming back?"

She jumped to her feet. "Oops, I totally forgot that there is an order waiting for me."

I shook my head at her and headed over to the blonde that wanted my attention. She was young, with huge hair and boobs. Her outfit made my waitress costume appear demure, and my feet ached when I looked at her feet crammed into six-inch heels with black straps wrapping around her calves up to her knees. The leather was tight enough that her skin bulged out between them, and one pinky toe appeared to be making an escape.

Opposite her was a middle-aged rotund gentleman wearing dark sunglasses. He belched loudly, and the aggressive odor of three-day-old garlic overwhelmed me. He looked me up and down slowly then licked his lips.

I fought the urge to run. "How can I help you?"

She looked up at me, and I realized she was much older than I thought, probably older than me. Her makeup sat heavily in the lines around her mouth and eyes. But even more so was the bitter, jealous, and mean emotions and energy flowing off her. Additionally, magic wafted off of her. It was sickly sweet like cheap perfume. It was probably meant to be sexy but made my stomach roll.

I was getting faster at pinpointing magic and emotions. I smiled to myself, but the man must have thought it was meant for him, as he broke into a broad smirk. His emotions and magic hung around him like stale cigarette smoke. I resisted the urge to step back and wave it away with a hand.

She winked at him. "We're going to have the lustful lemon chocolate cake."

He chuckled. "You're welcome to join us, doll."

It took me a second to realize he was talking to me. I gave him an anemic smile that was mostly teeth. "I'll get that for you." I practically ran to the door.

Patagonia jumped off her chair and bounded along next to me as I went into the hallway and stooped to shudder from head to toe like a dog throwing water off a wet coat. "Gross, gross, gross." I made a gagging motion. I continued down the hallway with an arm out to push open the left swinging door. "If a creepy man ever asks you—"

Halfway through pushing the door open, I felt sudden resistance then heard the sound of crashing plates and Vanessa's shrill scream.

I gently pushed open the swinging door to the right and peeked in. Vanessa was covered in nachos, and had a cheese-smeared plate and several now empty glasses at her side. "Did I do that?

She burst into laughter, shaking her hands and sending blobs of cheese everywhere with each flick.

The windows to the various kitchens were full of people curious as to the source of the noise, and a few seconds later, Isadora stormed out the door before pulling up short in shock.

"My kitchen! What happened?"

Vanessa was on her back, clutching her stomach with laughter.

I shrugged. "I'm sorry. We collided. It was an—"

"That's why there are two doors!" Isadora's face was turning an alarming red, and a vein at one temple was throbbing. The subtle strumming of magic was building. "You go in one and out the other. Idiots! I don't care what kind of investigation you're running, but if you even step a toe out of line, I'm kicking you both out and banning you for life. You got that?"

Everyone stared at us with increased fascination. So much for being undercover.

Vanessa was still giggling, so I kicked her, not too hard but enough to get her attention. She attempted to look serious, though the corners of her mouth kept curling up as she talked. "I'm sorry, Isadora. I'll be good."

Isadora's eyes narrowed. Skepticism and white-hot anger were rolling off of her. Hate was starting to solidify. "Go clean yourself up. I'm going to speak to your mother."

Vanessa sighed dramatically, either unaware or not caring about Isadora's growing hatred and the magic building around her. "Fine." She trudged out a door as a worker slid new drinks and nachos onto the window.

Isadora spun around at the noise, and everyone ducked out of sight. She jabbed a finger at the plate and drinks resting in the window. "Deliver those right away."

"Of course, right away. And when I get back, I'll put in this order." I moved over to grab the plate and moved the drinks carefully on my tray, jumping when she yelled again.

"Give me that order." She snatched the order pad off my tray. "You can't even write down orders correctly. And get that cat out of here. I don't care if she's magical or not. If I find a single cat hair in this room, the cleaning bill for the whole restaurant will come from your pay."

She banged on the bell at Beth's dessert window while I practically ran into the hallway. I checked that Patagonia was behind me and opened the door to the betting lounge wide so she could race ahead.

I didn't know where the order belonged, but the number of drinks and the only group with the same number of people swinging around to look when I entered the room made it an easy guess.

I apologized for the delay as I delivered the food then raced back to pick up the next order. I kept Patagonia in the hall and tentatively poked my head into the kitchen. It was empty, not even a head poking out of a window, except for a plate with a slice of chocolate cake in the window.

The cake needed to be delivered quickly, so I grabbed it and double-timed it back to the lounge, Patagonia racing ahead then stopping right in front of me. "No tripping me, silly cat. I've had enough drama for one day."

The top of the cake was so smooth that it reflected each light of the betting lounge. Surrounding the slice were red rose petals. The texture of the interior was smooth, more a ganache than a flour-based cake, and the rich chocolate scent tickled my nose. My mouth watering and stomach growling, I realized I had forgotten lunch and had only the barest of breakfasts. I felt weak, meaning I probably needed more sugar. Maybe I could order a slice of my own after this shift.

I slapped a smile on my face and placed the cake in front of the couple. "Here you go. Lustful Lemon. Enjoy!" I turned to go but was interrupted.

"Excuse me! This is not lemon. Look, there are rose petals. It's roses of remembrance. How dare you bring this?" the woman screeched.

I turned around and jumped when I realized she was inches from my face. I leaped back, and she shoved the plate at me.

Leaning forward to get her face back into mine, she lowered her voice. "I know you did this on purpose to remind him of his dead wife, so back off. He's all mine."

Patagonia hissed at her, baring her teeth.

The woman looked at her and hissed in response before slapping a fake smile on her face and bending over to grab the man's arm. "Come on, Eddie. We should go to the show to make sure we get the best seat. We can get some cake later."

I pursed my lips and spun around to return to the kitchen. I would not make a scene. I stormed through the hallway but remembered to carefully open the correct door into the kitchen. Inside, Vanessa was all cleaned up.

"Wow, that was fast." I looked her over. "How did you get the cheese out? You're not even damp."

She rolled her eyes. "Duh, magic. Why do you have a cake?" She edged closer and licked her lips. "It smells really good."

"I screwed up the order, and the chick accused me of doing it on purpose to make her date think of his dead wife. People are nuts."

"Was that that trampy blonde, Cynthia, with Eddie VanGuard?" She went over to a table covered with utensils that we sent out with each order.

"Could have been. She was definitely a trampy blonde, and she did call him Eddie."

She pulled a fork off the table and came back. "Eddie is a rich politician, and Cynthia was his wife's nurse. She's been trying to get a ring on her finger since the wife died, but I don't think Eddie is interested." She cut off the point of the cake and lifted it to her mouth.

"What are you doing? We can't eat it." I lifted the plate away from her.

"We have to. We can't screw up again, and bringing back an expensive piece of cake because you mixed up the order will get us in so much trouble. The magic is already running out, so they can't resell it later. I'm starving and need sugar, but most of all, I am missing Dad this week. He wouldn't make me study all day and night."

I had been following her logic until the last one. "What does your dad have to do with it?"

"It's remembrance cake. It thins the barrier between the living and dead just a tiny bit so you can feel the love of all those who have crossed over. Not much at all, because that is dangerous, but it's enough." Her eyes got a little shinier. "Don't you miss your dad?"

"Fine." I handed her the plate and went to get a fork. "But we don't tell anyone." I sliced through the smooth texture with the fork and scooped it into my mouth.

The chocolate instantly assaulted my senses with smooth, rich flavors. The sugar hit my bloodstream, and I starting feeling stronger. But the biggest thing was the tingly wave the flowed over me. It was warm and loving as memories of all the wonderful times with my father flooded my mind. Every trip, every phone call, every gigantic bear hug came flooding into my mind, and I was filled with his love for me, his only daughter. I knew that not only had he loved me, but that wherever he was, he still did.

I took another bite and caught Vanessa's eyes as a tear slipped down my face.

She sniffled and wiped her eyes. "Good, huh?" She took another bite.

"What are you doing!" Isadora screamed, her voice bouncing off the room, which was steadily rising in temperature.

I paused, my mouth full and the half-eaten cake on the plate in my hand. I swallowed hard, the mouthful painfully making its way down my throat. "The order was wrong."

Isadora stared so hard I thought she was going to burn a hole right through my face. "Orders that are wrong go back to Beth's table so she can harvest the magic. They are *not* eaten."

Vanessa finished off the bit on her fork. "If it's such a big deal, I can pay for it."

If anything, that infuriated Isadora even more. "This is my kitchen, and when you are here, you follow my rules. If I ever—" She cut herself off then pointed beyond us. "I want them out of here."

I turned slowly, dreading what was behind me. Vin loomed in the doorway to the hall, looking like a thunderstorm. The anger rolling around the room was building to such a high level that I resisted the urge to fan my face from the heat.

His fists were balled so tight that each knuckle stood

out white. "What are you doing?"

I quaked and tried to will myself to answer, when I realized his glare was not on me as I'd expected, but directed fully at his sister.

She squirmed under his stare, and her cheeks turned red.

Isadora turned all her wrath on Vin. "Get them out of here. Now!" The walls quaked under her building anger.

Vin grabbed his sister's arm and frog-marched her out the swinging door and into the hallway, stopping short of entering the betting lounge. I followed behind but at enough of a distance to be out of the immediate splash zone of his anger.

He turned his sister to face him. "What are you doing down here? Why are you wearing that?"

She avoided his glare. "I'm investigating. I'm… I'm undercover." She mumbled the last part.

"You're what? I told you to get Olivia or Mom to come down here."

She jutted out her chin defiantly. "Neither of them wanted to come. They're busy. I wanted to, and I did a great job. Didn't I, Ella?"

I held up my hands. This was one fight that had nothing to do with me, and I was not about to get in the middle.

Vin never took his eyes off his sister. "This is dangerous. There's a killer somewhere."

"I know it's dangerous, but you are letting Ella investigate, and she doesn't know anything."

"No one questions that." He jabbed a finger in my direction. I was tempted to defend my honor, but that didn't seem like the right time. "But you're my sister. I have to protect you. I promised Dad." He said the last thing slowly, imploring her to understand.

"Dad never wanted me to live walled away in a castle. We used to talk about all the fun, exciting things I would do when I grew up. He knew I wanted a purpose. What's the point of all my training if I can never use it? If he was here, he would... he..." She sniffed loudly, and tears started trickling down her face.

Vin reached out and enclosed her in a gigantic hug.

She sobbed into his shoulder as the tension in the hallway lowered.

He awkwardly patted her back as if he were trying to dislodge a piece of food stuck in her throat. "What did you do to Isadora? I've never seen her like that."

She sniffled and stepped back. "We ate a piece of cake, and she had a total cow."

"You weren't messing around with Beth's cakes, were you? Come on, Vanessa. You know they can be addictive."

My ears perked up. "*What?*"

Vin look startled, as though he had forgotten I was there. "You too? Be careful. We get cake junkies from time to time, but Beth is very good. She would never overdose you, but if you buy black-market cake, you can end up dying. It is pretty powerful magic. Now what did you learn?"

I shrugged. "Nothing. There was some excitement and anticipation, but overall, things were pretty mellow. Other than Isadora losing her mind. She was pissed, but nowhere else was anything weird."

"Nothing? Not even some sneakiness?" he said with a glimmer of a smile around his mouth.

I chuckled. "Not even that. What's next?"

Vanessa wiped her face. "Inhibition?"

Vin spun around to face his sister. "No, no, no. You're *not* going." He had gone a little white in the face and waved his hands side to side to cut her off.

She stomped her foot. "Yes, I *am*. You can't stop me."

They stood glaring at each other.

I cleared my throat. "What's Inhibition?"

CHAPTER SIXTEEN

I delivered pot stickers and draft beers to three gentlemen sharing a table in the back row. The show was set to start in a few minutes, then I would need to be more discreet about serving. I grabbed a quick order from a bachelorette party of five already tipsy women then went to put in the order.

The theater had rows of tables rather than seats. Each row was on its own level, and the tables only had seats along the back side so no one's view would be obstructed. Meals and drinks would be served throughout the show.

I looked behind me to find Patagonia, as had become my habit, then remembered that Vin had forcefully suggested she go home. One second she had been diligently cleaning between her toes, and when I turned back, she was gone. He assured me that she was fine, and if I was just a bit stricter, she would stay home.

I got in line behind Vanessa. "I didn't get why Vin was so freaked out about you being here." I looked to the far back corner where Vin had parked himself. He radiated grumpy energy, and the people at the table nearest him had asked to pay any amount to upgrade to a different table.

His protests in the hall had mostly focused on how

dangerous it was, but there was an undertone I couldn't place. Even my attempts to read the emotions had left me confused. Rather than fear and anger, as I had expected, he seemed to mostly feel embarrassed.

When neither Olivia nor his mother, Auntie Ann, had been free to help, he had relented but insisted we stay close, and only if a waitress was willing to take the night off.

As luck would have it, Natasha was assigned to the show and was happy to take the rest of her shift off, especially when Vanessa slipped her all the tips she had collected in the betting lounge.

Vanessa turned around and raised an eyebrow. "Have you been to Inhibition before?"

"No. I told you I hadn't even heard of it until now. I know Tiffany's in it." I gagged myself with a finger. "I assume it's one of those acrobat shows or something."

She gave me a big smile. "Yep, exactly. Don't like Tiffany?"

"You didn't hear! She attacked me this morning because she thought your brother and I were dating."

"That sounds like her. She's crazy jealous and just plain crazy."

I waited while she put in her order, then I added my own. The music started to get louder as the lights dimmed.

I followed her to the back corner opposite Vin, where we could see the window where we picked up food and all our tables. They had a button at each table that glowed red when they wanted to place an additional order. A couple worked their way up with an usher's help to the empty table next to Vin.

The deep bass of the music rattled my chest, and a sensual female voice rose in wordless vocals and the curtain slowly rose. A row of female dancers were strongly backlit so only their black silhouette was visible. They either had elaborate headdresses on or had feathers for hair. I was betting on the headdresses. In unison, they locked their arms onto their neighbors' shoulders and started kicking like a chorus line.

The room was filling with a variety of emotions from excitement to pleasure, but my cheeks burned red with the rising sensation of lust that had surged along with the music. The dozen ladies on stage were shapely, but the level of sexual emotions seemed a bit much.

The lights shot up, and I gasped. Every one of those women was topless, with only the barest of bejeweled thongs covering only the minimal landscape of their lady garden.

Twenty-four perfectly shaped, plentiful breasts bounced and jiggled in time to the high kicks and dance steps of the gorgeous women on stage.

They dropped their arms and spun off stage as the music changed to a jazzy number as the lights went dark again.

I had no idea how long they had been dancing. Their bosoms must have hypnotized me. I understood why Vin had been hesitant to have his sister here and why he had so deliberately parked himself as far away as he could get while watching over us.

When the lights went up, a single figure stood on the stage, two large feather fans in her hands. Even before she started dancing, I knew it was Tiffany. Her energy of heavy seduction over a veneer of anger was the same as this morning when she had kissed Vin goodbye. Flicking a fan just fast enough to cover herself but slow enough that we could tell she was nude, she spun and danced.

Her eyes were trained on the upper corner opposite us.

"Uh-oh. She knows Vin is here," Vanessa whispered in my ear.

Tiffany was pushing out enough sensual magic that I was sure everyone in the place was tingling in their nether regions.

The person at the window gestured to me that the food

was ready for one of my tables. I stepped over to take the food and found myself weak at the knees and fanning myself to cool down. I was going to need to tell Vin that I needed to leave and clear my head after I delivered the food to the table second from the end.

I carefully weaved my way past the other tables, where several couples weren't even attempting to be discreet as they pawed at each other. I started unloading the food to a table of two couples when a set of fingers pinched my behind.

With a scream and a jump, I lurched away, flinging the tray and the food still loaded heavily on top onto the table at the end.

A woman screamed, and a man started shouting, but I was trying to fight off a pair of hands that slipped around my waist and lips that were slobbering on my neck.

I screamed as I pressed against my assailant with both hands, but he refused to budge, other than his hands, which roamed over my stomach. "Get off me."

The lights came on, and the sickening thud of fists against flesh led to the weight and hands being lifted off me. The dazed gentleman was in Vin's fists, being shaken like a rag doll. Two other security guards were attempting to peel Vin off the man.

I rubbed my forehead. The emotions swirling around made me nauseated, and after a few moments of gagging, everything in my stomach wrenched out and landed on a familiar six-inch heel with lacing digging deep into a fleshy calf.

"Gross! Eww! It's you!"

I followed the leg up to the woman that I had met and offended in the betting lounge—Cynthia and Eddie VanGuard. She and her date were covered in the appetizers I had spilled when I had been accosted, and her shoes with covered with masticated remembrance cake.

I smiled. Thank heaven for small favors. If anyone deserved it, they did. The woman lunged at me, but a security guard grabbed her around the middle and dragged her away.

Vanessa grabbed my arm. "What happened?"

"I was going to ask you the same thing." For the millionth time that day, I was shaky on my legs, and I struggled to make sense of what had happened. "I was about to deliver some food when someone grabbed and groped me." I shuddered against the violation of being touched.

Vanessa ran a hand over my back. "If it helps, he didn't mean to. Tiffany must still be feeling insecure, because she was pumping out so much magic that she got half the room lust drunk."

I spun around to face the stage.

Tiffany was shrugging on a robe as Vin towered overhead, shouting at her. It was too far to hear the words, but his body language combined with his emotions surging across the room confirmed that he was angry. His anger was red-hot and a sensation that I was getting used to already. Feeling it was starting to be a comfort. I knew he was close and, like a bear, he would run down whatever was in his way.

Security guards were swarming in the room, and more poured in from a door that I hadn't seen before on the side of the theater. Three of them were detaining the couple I had spilled food on. The gentleman was grimly rubbing food from his clothing with a napkin, but the woman was glaring at me and pulling to get away from a man holding her arm.

"Let me at her. She did this on purpose. Yes, you! I see you looking!" the woman screamed, specks of spittle gathering in the corners of her mouth.

Vanessa pulled me away. "Ignore Cynthia. She's a loon. Come on. Let's get out of here."

I hobbled along, rubbing my lower back with a hand. "I feel like I've been hit by a truck." How many times had I fallen in the last twenty-four hours?

Vanessa nodded. "You're pretty clumsy, aren't you?"

I stopped. "No. Either I'm being attacked by a nut or tripped by a cat or some other such disaster. This is not normal." I leaned over briefly to rub a throbbing knee.

"Don't worry about it. I can help you with some magic when I grab my bag from the locker room." She offered me her arm.

We headed down the stairs as I leaned on Vanessa until we met up with Vin near the door.

He looked me over. "What a cluster. Did you get anything?"

I stared at him for a few counts before I remembered the purpose of being here. "I made some new enemies but nothing to help our investigation."

His eyes narrowed as he walked alongside me out the door of the theater. "Enemies? Who should I keep an eye on?" He scanned the attendees now gathering at the door of the theater.

"No one. I actually offended them earlier when I screwed up their order, then when I tripped, I spilled food on them. Then I threw up on her shoe. I've been busy." Thinking back to the surprise I found in my shoe this morning, I wondered if Patagonia was rubbing off on me.

"I see." He looked around at the bedlam of angry or confused patrons and the security guards milling among the crowd. "Why don't you two go change out of the uniforms. I'm not sure if we learned anything valuable today, but before I can debrief you, I need to deal with this. We need to cleanse the humans and give them a good cover story to believe, then we need to give rebates to the mages. I'll get everything settled and meet you outside the locker room."

I started to turn away, when Vin stopped me with a noise somewhere between a grunt and a cough. I faced him and waited while he struggled to get out what he wanted to say.

"Hey, Ella, you were right about those three guys. They

141

were running a scam, but you caught them. They are on a one-way flight out of town and will be banned from every magical establishment in the city. You did good this time."

"Thanks, Vin." Vanessa and I headed to the elevator. I felt as if I had been through a marathon, but Vanessa bounced along.

"That was so exciting. Investigating with you is so much more fun than with Mom or Olivia. They were going to get a huge whiteboard and list all the facts like you see in a movie." She pressed the button on the elevator and rubbed her neck. "That's so boring. I much prefer to be out here, getting my hands dirty, and—" She stopped and cocked an ear.

The elevator door opened, and I stepped inside as a voice overhead announced, "Vanessa Russo, please come to a white courtesy phone. Vanessa Russo to a white courtesy phone."

She rolled her eyes. "Probably Mom. I'll catch up."

"Sure thing." I grabbed a card from my pouch and slid it in the slot before I pressed the button to the floor with the locker room then leaned over to undo the buckle on my shoe. I would rather be barefoot than in those torturous heels even a second longer. I grabbed them by their straps and stood up.

Immediately, I swayed, little black dots swimming in my vision, and I reached out to clutch the handrail, but my hand slammed against it and fell off. My arms and fingers were heavy, the shoes slipping from my grip. There was a great rushing noise that several counts later I realized was my labored breathing. I lurched forward and fell, unable to break my fall as my head bounced off the floor.

Patagonia meowed and scratched my arm, the skin splitting open, bleeding but painless. The elevator stopped, and the doors opened, but I couldn't move. Unconsciousness called to me, and it seemed so easy and painless to just close my eyes and sink into it.

A primal voice in my head screamed that there was

danger, that I couldn't close my eyes, but that didn't make sense. I was alone and so tired. My raspy voice filled my ears as my breath caught in my throat. I couldn't pull in a breath at all anymore, but that didn't bother me. I didn't need to breathe. I just needed to close my eyes and rest.

The seer's voice came to me—"You are more powerful than you know, even without training"—while close on the heels was my father's love. I pushed all my magic into breathing, and a shaky breath tore from my lungs. I pushed off the floor and hauled my body partially through the door of the elevator as the door started to shut.

Patagonia yowled and ducked into my line of sight, as hazy as it was. She bit my hand, and I pushed again, dragging my body a few more inches out of the elevator. It became my whole world, fighting to breathe, pushing and dragging my body out of the elevator while Patagonia snipped at me and cried.

It might have been years, for all I knew, but eventually I must have cleared the elevator, because the door stopped closing on me. My whole world narrowed down to just that moment. That breath. I labored on through the moments, one after another, hoping that the next breath would be easier, but I continued to fight for each.

Patagonia stopped biting my hand, and two strong arms scooped me up like a baby.

From a great distance, or so it sounded, Vanessa sobbed. "I'm so sorry. I didn't mean to leave you. Vin, help her."

Large hands cradled my face and turned me to face him. "What happened?"

I focused on breathing in and out, not that I had a clue what to say if I could answer him.

He rushed somewhere, still carrying me, and carefully set me down. Looking into my eyes, he brushed some hair from my face. "You'll be fine. We've got you."

I believed him despite the fact that I felt a new emotion from him—fear.

CHAPTER SEVENTEEN

When I woke up on my bed at midnight, I was sore all over, my throat was on fire, and I was still exhausted. Patagonia was curled up against my neck, her purring audible. I was still in the waitress outfit, on top of the sheets, with all my possessions I had taken to the casino in a bag at my side.

I desperately wanted to keep sleeping, but after a few minutes of flopping around and attempting to find a comfortable position, I decided to get up for a bit. As I moved, every inch of my body ached.

Peeking out the bedroom door, I spied two of the security guards playing cards in my living room. They were here on Vin's order. Everything since stepping into the elevator was a blur, but some things were clearer than others. I had faded in and out of awareness, if not consciousness, as Vin barked orders. Auntie Ann and Olivia had been there at some point. Patagonia had meowed the whole time, my anchor to reality until someone drove me to my house and deposited me on my bed. I hadn't moved until now.

I was starving, but first I wanted to change. I slipped off the waitress outfit and rubbed my skin where the gold panties had dug deeply into my flesh. I dropped the outfit in a heap and grabbed a pair of flannel pajamas, old and soft from many washings, then a huge terry cloth robe. While I was in the closet, I grabbed a quilt from the top shelf.

I had made it for my dad when I was in junior high sewing class. It was black and white and made up of hundreds of triangles. They should have been right triangles, but due to my impatience at that age and my lack of skill, most were crooked, and some had extra sides. I had forgotten even making it until I cleaned out his closet and found it carefully folded on the top shelf.

I put the blanket on the bed and changed. The bedroom was small, with a large door that rolled on a track like a barn door. The space was big enough for the bed, large walk-in closet, and bathroom. It was meant to give a bit of coziness in the otherwise open-air loft. Besides a chair in the corner, the only other piece of furniture was a bookcase.

I had carefully placed the chest with the note from my father on a shelf next to a picture of us in France. While the shelves held many leather-bound books, there were also mementos of our trips together. Bundles of postcards we had written describing our adventures, framed photos, and small items that I couldn't resist buying. Next to the photo was an old copy of *Les Miserables* by Victor Hugo.

I felt the urge to hold it and sat on the bed to look it over. We had seen the musical several times, and I had even attempted to struggle through reading it. I wasn't sure how much I had read before I gave up and instead just listened to the soundtrack on repeat.

Through discussing the story, I had learned a lot about what type of person my dad was. Specifically my father's appreciation of Jean Valjean refusing to allow another man to go to jail in his place. I had felt that Jean Valjean had turned his life around and so many people depended on him, it didn't seem fair that he was held accountable for stealing bread for his starving family.

My father had explained that there would always be an excuse not to do the right thing. You had to commit to doing the right thing even when no one but you and God would know. If you started making excuses for the big things, slowly, there would be excuses for the little things.

I had seen this attitude demonstrated by my father a thousand times. Whether it was returning hours later to give back money when the street vendor had given our change back with a twenty instead of a five, or helping to change a tire even in the pouring rain, he always took the time. He had returned wallets and purses to their owners and stopped many a pickpocket theft.

It was obvious now that his ability as a mage helped him see things that others missed, but he could have chosen to look the other way.

I turned the book over in my hand and opened up the cover, and a card fluttered out.

Inside the birthday card was a cheesy joke and a brief note. "May this year treat you well. We're proud to fight with you. Justice is on our side. Your friends, Bear and Badger."

I put the card back inside and slid the book back on the shelf. I should read it one of these days. Turning around, I startled and covered my heart. Aristotle was on the bed, grooming Patagonia. If Aristotle was here, that meant Vin wasn't far behind.

After tying up my robe and putting my feet into slippers, I rolled open the bedroom door. Vin was closing the front door, and the security guards were gone.

He caught my eye as he locked the door, a pile of belongings at his feet. "I'm going to stay the night. No argument."

"No argument." My throat was rough, and the words squeaked out. "What did you find out?" I strolled out to the couch and flopped down.

Patagonia and Aristotle came running in and dove

headfirst into a bag.

Vin grabbed the bag, shooing out the cats and carrying it to the kitchen. "No argument? Are you feeling okay?"

"Actually no, and that's why I don't mind you being here. Please tell me you brought food."

He chuckled. "Yes, I did." He went into the kitchen and started pulling out cartons of food and grabbing plates.

I watched him. He was very comfortable in my kitchen, in my home. "Tell me what you know." I pulled a blanket over my legs as I curled up with my feet underneath me and leaned over the back of the couch to watch.

He poured pasta in a thick white sauce into a bowl. "We haven't been able to find out who paged Vanessa, but clearly it was so you would be in the elevator alone. You were targeted." He came out of the kitchen to hand me the bowl.

"And?" I twirled a fork and pulled up long fettuccine noodles. The thick, creamy sauce had more than a touch of garlic. I couldn't help letting out a little moan of pleasure.

"And we don't know a lot more than that. That message kept Vanessa from joining you. There was a nasty little curse set up like a mousetrap. It went off when you got in. We were going to comb the footage, but it looks like everyone and their mom used that elevator, and they might have used a disguise."

I finished off the bowl and reached for a peach cobbler that Vin brought over. "Am I okay? I mean will there be any permanent damage?" I winced a bit as I swallowed the crumbly crust.

"Magically, you're fine. Mom made sure of it. Physically, you're a bit beat up but should be better in a day or two. You did good, you know. That really should have killed you, but you fought it."

"Thanks. Life-and-death really brings out the fighting spirit." I grabbed some garlic bread and a few olives.

"Basically everyone in the casino knows you're investigating for us, and the killer has guessed what you're investigating. Taking that into consideration, along with the attack, we've decided to take you off this case. I'll stay the night to make sure nothing more happens, but tomorrow you'll stay here with some bodyguards. We'll still pay you, both the money and the information about your father. And Mom still wants to train you, but this is just too dangerous."

"What about the murderer?"

"Maybe they will quit." He poured two glasses of wine then grabbed his plate off the coffee table.

"Not if they tried to kill me. If they were going to quit, they would have just disappeared."

"Fine, then we'll catch them. Don't worry about that. You'll get paid."

I chewed my bread and grabbed a glass of red wine and took a sip. I could walk away. It would be safer, and I could start my search for Bear and Badger. It wasn't my fault that someone could die tomorrow if we didn't find the killer. But was that what my dad would do? Was that something I could live with?

The killer had targeted me, so clearly we were getting close. Maybe I had seen or done something that made them think I was a risk. If I was the only one that was in danger, could they find the killer without me?

"No," I said then finished off the glass to steady my nerves for what I was doing. "I'm not staying home tomorrow. I'm going, and we'll catch the killer together."

"You'll be safer here."

"You don't think you can protect me?"

"Of course I can, but..." He stared out the window, scrunching his eyebrows up in thought. His emotions had been tightly under control, but just the slightest hints were creeping out. He was pleased and proud. "Fine. We'll go in together tomorrow." He stood up and grabbed the empty plates and glasses.

"That's it? I figured you would argue with me." I twisted around to watch him as he put everything into the dishwasher.

"It's your neck." He turned off the lights in the kitchen and went to grab his bags by the door. "Go to bed. You need your rest. Sleep as long as you can. It will help you heal. When you get dressed, pick out something that is your favorite. Something that makes you feel in control and powerful."

"We having a fashion show?"

"Why don't you just trust me, eh? How you feel affects your magic, and you need every bit of help you can get. You were close with your dad, right? Wear something he gave you. That'll help. And sleep with your channel stone, and make sure to bring it."

I nodded along. I had already slipped on the necklace my dad had left for me, but I had some earrings and rings I could add. "Anything else?"

"If you're at all religious, you might consider praying, because tomorrow we are going to need every bit of help we can get."

CHAPTER EIGHTEEN

The next day, I sat in the employee conference room and did my best to look engaged. The white boards all around the room were covered with information about the victims that told us nothing concrete. So far, we had nothing that seemed to get us any closer to finding the murderer or how they did it.

Since Vanessa and I were banned from Isadora's Ristorante, we didn't meet in the Ristorante at a table with a full-time waiter, but instead the bland and foodless room across from the locker room.

Coming down the elevator before the meeting, I had hesitated until Vin assured me that there were no curses this time.

When I arrived at the meeting, Olivia, Vanessa, and Auntie Ann had fussed over me a bit before we settled down to comb through the massive amount of information we had collected. As an accountant, I should have been used to the task, but instead I felt antsy and struggled to focus.

The amount of data they had gathered was overwhelming, but almost nothing seemed to be consistent between the five besides the locations we already investigated. Two were born in March, but the rest throughout the year. Two worked in a casino, but not the other three. All five had used the same elevator, but so had virtually every employee and visitor to the casino, plus we had checked it over several times and couldn't find anything.

I was badgered by the feeling that I was missing something important. I specifically had been targeted, so the murderer had seen or heard of something I had done that they felt put them at risk. That seemed like a given, but what? Maybe they were mistaken and thought I was smarter or more talented or skilled than I was. Or perhaps...

I fidgeted with my rings, spinning them around my fingers. I had on every bit of jewelry I could get away with, all gifts from my father, especially the necklace he had left for me. It was the most meaningful, though the exact meaning I had yet to discover. Perhaps Bear and Badger would be able to help me discover what my father had wanted to tell me.

I had finished off my outfit with tight jeans that were as soft as butter and cut perfectly to cover my butt even when I squatted. A simple fitted thermal top with funky metal buttons on the cuffs and knee-high leather boots finished off the outfit. Tucked into my cleavage and out of sight was the channeling stone.

Patagonia purred contentedly in my lap. I hadn't even attempted to leave her at home. Occasionally, she would delicately chew on my fingers, hard enough for me to wince but not enough to break the skin. It was as if she wanted me to know who was in charge.

I had to admit that I did feel a bit more in control dressed in my favorite outfit, and the appreciative glance from Vin that I caught in the reflection of the car as we left hadn't hurt either.

"Perhaps we should break for lunch. Some of us seem to be losing focus," Auntie Ann said, looking right at me.

"Sorry, I'm still tired." I forced a yawn.

She didn't buy it, gauging by her chuckle. "It's fine. One of the only things we can say for sure is that all the murders happened between midnight and three a.m. I have a great deal of faith that we will solve this before the next one occurs." She smiled radiantly, but no emotion was coming off of her.

She had taught me a simple shielding spell that morning. It would help protect me from magic coming in and emotions and spells coming out. It had to be constantly maintained, and it appeared she was doing just that, making me wonder exactly what emotions she was hiding.

We stood up and exited into the hallway, set to go to lunch, when we ran into Natasha leaving the elevator in her waitress uniform.

"Ella!" she called out, waving.

I broke away from the group as they discussed where to eat. "Hey Natasha. You just finish a shift or about to start one?"

She shrugged her bag higher onto her shoulder. "Just finishing. Are you guys going to eat as a group, or are you free?" Vanessa came up alongside.

"You can come too, Vanessa. The more the merrier."

I turned back to the group and caught Vin's eye. He must have been listening because he nodded. "You're free to go, and I think I will join you."

I resisted the urge to roll my eyes at him, but I didn't want to tip Natasha off that his joining was anything other than just a casual lunch get-together. "Great. Where do you want to eat? I'm open to anywhere."

Vanessa giggled next to me. "Except Isadora's Ristorante. We're banned for being lousy waitresses."

Natasha's eyes grew wide. "Wow, you must have been really terrible. Don't worry about going there. I saw they were closed today. Hopefully that means Beth will take a day off finally. She's had such a terrible few months." She shook her head sadly.

I aimed for a casual tone with a hint of concern. "Oh no, how awful. What happened?"

"Two of her closest friends died. They were all part of the same crowd that hung around outside of work."

An excited buzz started to build in my stomach. "I think I heard something about two employees dying, but I didn't realize Beth knew both of them."

"She actually dated both of them. She and Michael had been childhood sweethearts, but they had a falling out. She and Tony had been on and off again for a while. But they all still hung out in the same group. They were all pretty young. You know how it is."

I nodded along, even though that was nothing like anything I had experienced. "How upsetting for Beth. I hope she rests."

"Me too. She works seven days a week because she can't trust anyone else to make those chocolate cakes, but with Isadora's closed, she can take a break."

The mention of chocolate cake reminded me of something. "It's not normally closed?"

"Nope."

An idea was swirling around in my head, but I needed a few minutes to talk it out. "Why don't you go change, and we'll grab lunch once you're done."

As she left for the locker room, I signaled everyone back into the room. The door was barely closed when I burst out. "Isadora's. Beth. The cake!" I ran over to the table, trying to find the tablet where I had viewed the footage from each of the accident scenes. I didn't ever want to see them again, but I had to remember.

"What is it, dear?" Auntie Ann asked, echoing the questioning looks on everyone's face.

"Where are the videos? I just made a connection. When I watched the video, right before they died, I felt this wonderful feeling, and I just recognized it when Natasha mentioned Beth. It's that cake I had, the one that reminds you of people you loved that passed."

Olivia grabbed the tablet from under a stack of papers. "Did you get that at every location?"

I was too excited to stand still and started pacing. Patagonia trailed behind me, meowing. "No, but I got nothing at all in the parking lot where Michael overdosed. And neither at Tony's, the blackjack dealer who was killed in the stables. All I got there was that poor horse. But the other three, there was this swell of happiness right before they did whatever it was that took their life. That has to be important, right? Didn't you say that the cake can kill you if done wrong?" I spun around to find Vin with the last question.

"Yes. Usually it happens right then, but I suppose…" He nodded thoughtfully.

Auntie Ann agreed. "Maybe using the cake with a delayed reaction or maybe…"

Finally, things were making sense. "What happens when people overdose on the cake?"

Auntie Ann sobered. "It is different per cake, but if you overdose on remembrance cake, or it is made improperly, you can… Oh yes, I see how that could work."

"What?"

"The spell in the cake thins the walls between the living and those that are no longer with us. We always have their love with us—death can't take that away—but the spell loosens the veil enough so we feel it even more. People have hurt or killed themselves when the spell is too strong They are so caught up that they walk into traffic. That is why the cake is served in supervised locations and you have to be very well trained. If part of the cake's spell was on a delay and they were lured somewhere dangerous, then—"

Vanessa bounced on her toes. "They could have stepped in front of a tram, or out a window, or into a horse's stall even though it was mad. That's it. Beth did it. We have to catch her."

"Calm down, sweetie." Auntie Ann patted her daughter's shoulder. "Olivia and I will find out where she lives, and then after lunch we can meet up and put together a plan. Why don't you three go with Natasha, see if you can get any more details out of her without being too obvious. I want everyone to get a lot of food—you'll need the energy—and be back in an hour."

CHAPTER NINETEEN

We met up with Natasha once she was done and got into the elevator.

She reached over and pressed the button for the third floor. "Why don't we go to the food court since you only have an hour. It'll be the fastest."

Vanessa scooted between Vin and me until she was next to Natasha. "I had no idea about Beth. So sad. Do you know her well?"

Natasha fidgeted awkwardly. "Kind of. I wasn't going to mention this 'cause Olivia is her boss and everything, but I think I should. They were all kinda mixed up in Legacy."

Vanessa gasped.

I leaned around her. "What's Legacy?"

Natasha blushed a little. "A magic-based drug. Michael had gotten clean last year, but Tony started dealing and got them all hooked again. Michael's mom was covering for him at work, but he was a real mess until they fired him. I wasn't really that surprised he overdosed in the parking lot. I was really sad but not surprised. Then Tony died around that horse, but he was great with animals—he grew up on a ranch—so I started thinking that maybe he had been

156

high. I told Beth to get help, and I thought she had because she was really shaken up by their deaths, but if she doesn't... Maybe someone should know. She doesn't have any family around here."

The doors chimed as they opened, and I followed Vin out. "Have you ever noticed—" I cut off suddenly when I ran into Vin's back.

He looked around. "This is the wrong floor." He spun around.

The elevator door was gone, only smooth wall in its place. A chill ran down my spine.

The elevator had opened directly onto an outside balcony suitable for hosting a party. The view of the city showed that we were at least four floors up, if not more. The balcony had a clear glass half wall along the edge, though a large section was missing. Standing at the edge were Beth and Isadora. Neither woman had noticed us yet. We were on the side of the casino that faced away from the Avenue. The outdoor options like lounge chairs, pools, and a swim-up bar were on this side, though no one would be out with the cold wind whipping around.

Vin scooped us over to the side to hide behind a large column.

Natasha looked around, alarmed. "What's going on?"

Vin took charge of the situation. "There isn't time to explain, but Michael and Tony's deaths weren't accidents. Someone has been killing people, and we think it is Beth, and it looks like Isadora is her next victim. We don't know a lot about the magic she's used, but I might be able to block the spell. You guys stay out of sight."

Vanessa grabbed his arm. "You can't go alone. We don't know what else is set up."

He wrestled mentally for a few seconds before relenting. "Fine. We can go, but Natasha and Ella will stay."

"No," Natasha said. "I'm her friend. Maybe I can talk to her."

The two women walked closer to the edge of the balcony and looked down, with nothing to hold them back from falling over or being pushed.

Vin handed me a blue stone egg, much like my channeling stone. "Stay here. Hold this."

I grabbed Patagonia and held her to my chest, praying that she wouldn't call attention to us.

The three of them stepped out from behind the pillar and carefully approached. Whether it was the way the wind blew or magic, I could hear everything.

Natasha was the first to speak. "Beth, honey, it's Natasha. What's going on?"

Beth turned around, her eyes wide and unfocused. Tears were streaming down her face, dragging mascara with them. They pooled at her chin and fell off. When she spoke, her voice was hollow and distracted. "Michael and Tony, they're here. They say I can come with them."

Vin snarled. "Son of a—No, Beth, it's not your time yet." He turned to Natasha and Vanessa. "We were wrong. Shield Beth."

Isadora let out a scream of frustration. "This doesn't concern you. Beth and I were just discussing my son."

Vin edged closer. "Yes, it does. We know everything."

"Leave me alone. I have the right to take my vengeance. She killed my son. She and her boyfriend got him hooked back on drugs. Stop, or I'll push her myself!" Isadora screamed.

Vin stopped and held up his hands. "Your son really did overdose, didn't he?"

"Tony and Beth killed my son, and their guilt over the loss will be their undoing."

"What about the two others? What did they do?"

"No one cares about them. They're just humans. But the casino deserves the bad press. You fired him. You also need to take responsibility for killing him."

Beth raised a hand toward the open space in front of her. "Tony?" She toddled on the edge.

Vanessa took a small step toward the edge, and her shaky voice rang out, airy and distracted. "Daddy?"

I could feel the same surge of love and warmth that I felt when eating the remembrance cake and on the video. Beth and Vanessa were deeply under its spell. The veil between the living and the dead was thinning, and they were being lured to their deaths. They had consumed the same spell I had yesterday.

I swallowed hard and fought off the growing emotions coming over me. I fought back tears as the thoughts of my father came over me.

Vin whispered under his breath. "I'm sorry, Ella." He rushed and hit Natasha, Beth, and Vanessa like a linebacker. All four of them disappeared over the edge, their screaming fading away.

I cried out in shock and fear. The elevator was still gone, the whole wall smooth. Perhaps it was an illusion and if I got close enough, I could feel the elevator and press the button. I was debating doing that when I was hit with a sensation so strong it could have been physical.

My father was here. I turned around, and his voice floated through the air from beyond the edge of the balcony. "Gabriella?"

A sob caught in my throat as I stumbled toward it. I dropped Patagonia, but the blue stone in my hand pulsed, and a burning-hot sensation grew in the center of my chest, bringing clarity to my head. I knew exactly what was happening, but I struggled to fight against it. Why would I? I could go to my father and be with him again. He could tell me what had happened, why he had never told me who I was.

The small part of my brain that was still unaffected screamed that he wouldn't want that, not yet. That I had a life ahead of me. That I had to find out who killed him. That I had to fight.

I used whatever strength I had to fight the magic around me. I built up the boundary to protect myself. As I did, the spell loosened its grip on me. My father's presence, the memories, and everything I loved about him faded away.

Isadora's eyes widened. She opened her mouth to speak, when her whole body jerked, and she whipped her head around to the open space beyond the balcony. "Michael?" She took an unsteady step to the edge of the balcony then stepped right off the edge, falling straight down without a sound.

I raced to the edge. Several floors below was a cement deck surrounding a pool. Leading from the pool were four wet trails to where Vin, Natasha, Beth, and Vanessa stood. Directly below lay Isadora, her broken form on the hard surface and a dark-red puddle growing around her head.

CHAPTER TWENTY

After Isadora died, the spell had broken, and security rushed out through the elevator to drag me from the edge of the balcony. I had been unable to move until they grabbed my arms and hauled me away.

Auntie Ann had checked me over. There was nothing magically or physically wrong with me, and after my begging, they let me drive home in the car I had left there the night before.

I had locked the door of the loft behind me then gone straight to my bed to sob until I fell asleep. Where the remembrance cake the day before had been a wonderful experience, what I had experienced on the balcony had felt like having my father back then losing him all over again. My heart had been torn open, my wounds fresh again.

When I awoke in the evening with Patagonia pressed to my chest, I had washed off the grime of the day. I got out of the shower that night, my hands and feet prune-like. I couldn't seem to get warm, no matter how long I let the hot water beat against my back as tears ran down my face. I had never seen someone die right in front of me, and after this investigation, I had more than enough images of death burned into my brain.

Slipping into my pajamas and slippers, I checked my phone right as the doorbell rang. On a hunch, I grabbed Vin's channeling stone off the bed and ambled over to the door. A quick check confirmed my suspicions, and I opened the door to Vin, who was carrying a paper bag.

"This is yours. What's it made of?"

He slipped the stone into his pocket. "Lapis. I needed to explain some things."

I opened the door and invited him in. Patagonia rubbed her nose against his knees as he walked, then sat down on the floor next to his feet to thoroughly sniff every inch of his shoes. He leaned down and scratched behind her head before continuing. "How are you feeling?"

I pulled my legs underneath me on the couch and grabbed a blanket to cover my lap. "Exhausted. Drained. Upset. Do you know when you jumped off that balcony, my heart stopped? I couldn't imagine why you did it."

"I'm sorry." He swallowed hard. They were clearly not words he often said. "Beth was seconds from stepping off the ledge, and Vanessa had gone from helping us fight Isadora to falling under her spell. Isadora had a huge advantage, and Natasha and I were losing. Natasha is very talented but not in that way. I knew if we landed in the pool, we would all be safe."

"How did you know you would make it and not splat on the cement? The water isn't that deep. You could have all broken your necks."

"You forget that I had magic to help us. I knew we would be fine."

"Why weren't you affected?"

"The cake you had the day before."

I tipped my head to the side, not expecting that answer. "The one that Vanessa and I ate after I screwed up the order?"

He shook his head. "You didn't screw up the order. Isadora purposefully put in the wrong order. When a slice of cake is returned, Beth absorbs back the energy magically, and the effect is similar to eating the cake herself. That was how Isadora had planned to get Beth to be the next target. But then you and Vanessa also ate the cake and were affected by the magic. Natasha and I weren't affected, but even working together, we were losing, and that's why I had to do what I did."

I avoided his eyes. "But what about me? You just left me there. You could have called me over, but instead you abandoned me."

"You were fine."

I whipped my ahead around to snap, "But you couldn't know that!"

"Yes, I *could*. I knew that I couldn't keep both Beth and Vanessa safe, but I was pretty sure you would be. Listen, you know that necklace you were wearing yesterday? The one your dad gave you?"

"How did you know that?" I reached up and felt the necklace under the robe, pulling it out so I could look at it.

"A few days ago when you flashed your cleavage at me, I saw it and recognized it. Your father made it to protect you. It won't protect you from everything, but like the channeling stone, it added some defense. The necklace is especially effective against magic that is intended to use your love for your father against you. Did you feel tempted to walk off that balcony?"

"I mean, a little, but…"

"Vanessa and Beth were seconds from flinging themselves off that ledge, and they have years more training than you. Didn't it seem strange that you could fight off the magic and they couldn't? You had Patagonia, the necklace, your channeling stone, and mine. If you could protect yourself from the spell, it would go to whoever was left—Isadora. Letting a spell like that loose is dangerous specifically because it can turn back on the spell caster, and it did. It was Isadora's own spell that compelled her to kill herself to be with her son. It was a risk to leave you up there but a calculated risk. And one I stand behind. You expected me to watch my little sister die right in front of me and not try to save her?"

I thought long about it. "No, you're right." I didn't feel great about his decision, but I couldn't argue anymore. I was hurt to be thought of as a calculated risk, but what did I expect? "Why didn't you tell me earlier?"

"I was busy. There is still a lot to do to clean up the situation. I wasn't going to say anything at all, but Mom asked me to because she thought it might affect us working together in the future."

"Why didn't you tell me that the necklace would help protect me from spells?"

"I thought you might be more cautious if you didn't know about it. It's also why I stuck so close when you waitressed. You didn't wear it that day."

I shrugged. "The rules said no jewelry, though if I had known it was magical, I would have broken the rules." I wasn't ready to put the whole issue behind us.

He ignored my jab and stood up, handing me a bag. "Here's food. Mom will be in touch next week to train you. I have to go."

I took the food and resisted the urge to kick him as I let him out the door.

A few minutes later, the doorbell rang again. Perhaps Vin regretted the way he handled things and wanted to apologize, but when I opened up the door, I saw that it was Lou Freeman and Mike Clinton from the two businesses on the floors below the loft. I had meant to call them in the morning.

I opened my mouth to apologize, when I recognized something that I hadn't before. Magic radiated off both of them. Lou Freeman was a tall, burly man with not only a massive beard and mustache, but hair all over like a bear. Mike Clinton was shorter but just as wide, with a grim determination like a badger. They had both worked with my father for decades from maintaining his car and security, plus they were the only people from Rambler that my dad had ever mentioned, even in passing.

I sighed. "You're not here about my alarm system or my car, are you?"

Mike shook his head. "No, Gabriella, we aren't."

I opened the door. "Come in. We have a lot to talk about."

ABOUT THE AUTHOR

Nikki Haverstock is a writer who lives on a cattle ranch high in the Rocky Mountains. She has studied comedy writing at Second City and has published 9 cozy mysteries that are heavy on the humor.

Before fleeing the city, she hosted a competitive archery reality show, traveled the world to study volcanoes, taught archery and computer science at a university and now works on her family's ranch herding cattle. Nikki has more college degrees than she has sense and hopefully one day she will put one to work.

Nikki likes to write comedy pieces that focus on the everyday humor of one-uppers, annoying family members and strange behavior of the ultra-rich. She tried stand up but the cattle weren't impressed.

Learn more about Nikki's other books and sign up for her newsletter at http://nikkihaverstock.com/

22798749R00100